A witch an
Can they w
they love?

Astrid, a Witch of the Ironwood, is content in her life. Her people live separately as a group of women who acknowledge no man's rule, using sorcery to conceal and protect themselves. When Astrid's vision quest reveals a quest with a warrior she has never met, she sets out to fulfill her destiny.

Huw is a Jomsviking, a legendary group of mercenary fighters whose reputation is both feared and admired. A ruthless warrior, he is used to having his every word obeyed without question.

Thrown together by a goddess with her own agenda, the witch and the warrior must find a way to defeat an ancient evil that has been resurrected. It threatens not only the Witches of the Ironwood, but to upset the balance of power forever. Each faces a dilemma. Astrid must choose between her beloved sisterhood and the warrior who commands her submission. Huw must decide between being a member of an ancient brotherhood and the woman who has captured his heart.

In an evil and dangerous world, a battle of passion and destiny.

Witch and Warrior

Viking Masters

Digital ISBN: 978-1-68361-550-7

Print ISBN: 978-1-68361-551-4
Cover art by Fantasia Frog

Published by Decadent Publishing Company, LLC
Look for us online at:
www.decadentpublishing.com

Hello! I'm Tom Rhymer, and what I love most in the world is to tell stories of adventure that will set your hearts racing. I invite you to escape with me, into worlds that are filled with bold heroes, daring heroines, duplicitous villains, and lots of healthy doses of good naughty fun.

I've been fascinated with the Age of Vikings since I was young, and have had a lot of fun working with Delta James to create a stirring adventure in a world I've loved for so very long. I hope you enjoy the saga of Astrid and Huw, two adventurers determined to save the things they love.

I hope that you enjoy this naughty adventure! You can contact me at tomrhymer1@gmail.com.

***

Thank you for reading ***Witch and Warrior!*** I hope you'll love it half as much as my buddy, Tom, and I did writing it. It's a bit of a departure from my paranormal shifters and BDSM, but I think you'll find all the elements you've come to expect in one of my stories.

When Tom told me his idea for this book and asked if I wanted to co-write it with him, I didn't hesitate for even a moment. Opportunities to work on an exciting project with a good friend don't come along very often. In fact, we had such a good time, that what started out as a stand alone project, became a trilogy. Look for ***Bone and Blade*** and ***Song and Sword*** coming in later this year.

If you enjoy this book, I would love if you left a review, they make a huge difference for authors. You can reach me at deltajames-author@hotmail.com or through my website www.deltajames.com. As always, my thanks to all of you for reading my books. Take care of yourselves and each other.

Dedication

To the ones who got me here

WITCH AND WARRIOR

by

Tom Rhymer

and

USA Today Bestselling Author

Delta James

Prologue

Kasia entered the clearing in the woods above their village. There, on the altar dedicated to Freyja, lay the warrior who had been stripped of his clothes, bound, and gagged. Her vision quest had shown her she was to carry a child of the next generation of witches; he was to be the sire of her baby. He had violated the boundaries of the Witches of the Ironwood. Punishment for trespass for brawny men with fair features was to be captured and prepared for their use. He was indeed handsome and well made; his muscles bulged and rippled as he struggled with his restraints.

The warrior's eyes grew large, their centers increasing in size, as she removed her clothing. As was the custom of the sisterhood, Kasia was completely without hair. Her naked flesh had been anointed with special oils. Sacred spells for conception had been drawn on her body, and her hair had been unbound, cascading all around her.

Kasia approached him, stopping to stand by his head. His gaze was fixed; he couldn't seem to take his eyes off her. Her nipples were pebbled from both the chill in the air and the knowledge she was to finally make her important contribution to the furtherance of the sisterhood. She reached up to roll and pinch her hardened tips with one hand as the other stole down her body, separating the folds of her sex to play briefly with the engorged nub that was her crown jewel. Kasia had already been preparing to take his cock up into her body. Her sheath was warm and wet in preparation for his penetration.

Gathering the feminine dew from her core, she removed his gag and forced her fingers past his lips, rubbing them along his tongue so he could taste her wild honey.

"Gods' teeth," he ground out. "Unbind me, woman."

"That I will not do, but do not fear, I have been instructed how to bring you pleasure in breeding." She looked down at his fully engorged and erect staff and smiled. "I was also told how to ensure you were hard enough for my use, but I can see that won't be a problem."

"I fear nothing, especially a comely wench like you, but if you think to ride me like a stallion, think again. Untie me. I was in search of a wife and, as you can see, I find you fair and buxom, and you will suit me well. I am Brynn of the Jomsviking. Our brotherhood is made of men of iron. Untie me now, and I will put you on your back and claim you as mine. Persist in this violation, and, when I return for you, before I claim you as mine in front of my men, I will see your backside covered in the red stain from my handprints."

Kasia liked the sound of his voice, even though she discounted his words. The men of the Jomsviking had long been considered prime breeders but failed to see being chosen as the gift and honor it was, choosing the life of the warrior over family. As he spoke, she rubbed her swollen nubbin and stroked her channel. She continued to play with herself until she was at the edge of release. Climbing up on the altar, she straddled his body.

"This is unholy," he said, "Release me now. I swear I will take you to my furs and claim you properly."

"But that is not our way," she said, indicating his prone body. "This is most proper for a Witch of the Ironwood. We are outside your society, and our sisters answer to no one but each other. It is a fair trade. I give you my cunt in exchange for your seed. When I am done with you, and before the sun next rises, I will cast a spell to keep you safe while you recover and sleep. Then I will release your bonds, and you can return to your people."

"I'm warning you, if you do this, I will pay you back in kind. You will be bound to our bed when I put the first of a series of babies in your belly. For each time you use me this night, I will take a strap to your bottom and leave a welt behind."

Kasia laughed as she trailed a finger down the center line of his body.

"Why is it men become incensed when they are used for their intended purpose and yet do not see forcing a woman to their bed in the same manner as wrong? Sex is sex—a means to an end, be it pleasure or procreation. I intend, Brynn of the Jomsviking, to see you have both this night."

Brynn's cock was large and ready for her use. As she hovered over him, his hips seemed to thrust upward as if of their own accord. The broad head parted the petals of her sex, and Kasia moaned. She could feel and see his staff throbbing in anticipation. She leaned against his chest and allowed her hair to cover his face. She was so wet and her nipples so hard.

Just as she began to lower herself onto his erect

phallus, he thrust his pelvis up, sending his cock straight to the end of her channel. He filled her completely; pleasure overwhelmed her, and she orgasmed, her honey coating his cock and making it easy for her to begin to ride him. As she rotated her hips, Brynn began to fuck up into her body. Kasia threw her head back, leaning back on her hands as he did it again and again.

Even though he was still bound, he thrust up into her, making her breasts bounce as she climaxed a second time. Kasia could feel his strength and dominance as he continued to move his cock in and out. She rode closer to another orgasm with each roll of his hips. She used him hard, feeling every inch of him as he drove deeper and deeper into her. He grimaced, and his body stiffened as she came again, and she felt him release his seed into her. Her pussy clamped down all along his length, milking him for every last drop.

When the storm was over, Kasia settled herself, flinging her hair behind her shoulders, feeling inordinately proud of herself. She had accomplished her goal. Now to see how long it would take him to recover before she could use him again. She opened her eyes and leaned forward to kiss him.

"You'll pay for that, witch," he hissed. "When I get you beneath me—and I will—I'll fuck you so hard, you won't be able to walk to the hall for the evening meal."

Kasia paid him no mind and rode him three times more before she cast a spell of protection and rest, hoping to ensure his seed would take root. Just before he drifted off to sleep, she leaned down to kiss the head of his spent manhood.

Brynn growled. "I'll teach you to suck my cock before I send my seed down your throat and into your belly. I'll claim your ass before I fuck your pussy again," he grumbled.

She ran her hands down his body. He really was very handsome. Listening to him snore, she untied him, picked up her clothes, and headed back to their village. The independence of the sisterhood would continue into future generations, thanks to encounters like these.

Chapter One

Four Months Later...

The offerings had been made; Astrid had begun her vigil. Drawing her cloak around her shoulders, she settled into her chair in front of the fire. Surprised that she didn't have to stand or even kneel, she listened to the others before they left her. Some of the older, more experienced witches had warned her the night would be long and hard.

"Remember, Astrid, that witches like comfort," one had said.

Another had added, "We know how to suffer, which means we also know when we don't have to."

The last to leave had been her friend, Kasia, who was close to Astrid in age. She had tried to lessen Astrid's concerns with her encouraging banter.

As she readied to leave, Kasia said with a warm smile, "Did you remember a blanket? The night can be cold, even with a fire." Astrid nodded. "Your vigil night can be hard, yes, but it can also be exhilarating. The *utiseta* can bring visions that define your path for many years to come." She placed her hand on her gently swelling belly. "Be open to the experience!"

The *utiseta*—her first night of sitting out alone, open to the will of the gods and goddesses—was upon her. Perhaps, finally, she would be shown a true path, or at least her purpose might become clearer. Gingerly, she picked up the wooden bowl beside her, which contained the sacred mushrooms, placed several in her mouth, and began to chew. Their strong, pungent taste was not pleasant. She puckered her lips and took a drink of water, before finishing the bowl.

"They will make you more open to the words of the gods," Kasia had explained.

"And the goddesses, more likely," Astrid had added.

Astrid was nervous, but the Witches of the Ironwood had been practicing *utiseta* for countless generations. It kept them close to the gods and goddesses, whose favor they called upon to preserve their independence from the world of men. She had seen other witches return from their night—changed, confident, renewed.

As she watched, the fire began to leap and twist in the air. Astrid narrowed her eyes. She questioned whether or not she could see actual faces or bodies dancing, writhing in wild abandon as they frolicked amongst the licking tongues of the flames.

The modest campfire appeared to have grown into a raging bonfire—an inferno that blazed around her with an army of the flaming giants encircling her, drawing and expelling their breath until they combined to become one single, connected creature.

Astrid's eyes widened. She dared not move.

Slowly, the fire that surrounded her began to recede. All that was left behind was a ring of ash...literally. Her chair, cloak ,and blanket had all disappeared. In fact, she realized with a shock that her clothes were missing as well. She was completely naked.

The cold night air should have left her freezing. Instead, Astrid felt enveloped by a warmth she knew to be not of this world. She heard a rustling in the undergrowth behind her. Startled, Astrid turned to see a man just outside the ring of ash, who stood and gazed at her appreciatively. He was tall, broad shouldered, and well-muscled. He reminded her of a warrior straight out of a saga. She faced him squarely, hiding nothing. She was proud of her body and, besides, this was her vision...not his.

He stepped into the ring to stand before her. The warrior took hold of her chin, tilting her head to look at him.

"Yes," the man said in a lustful tone as he ran his finger down the column of her throat. "Yes. You are exactly what I desire."

Astrid felt mesmerized, and her body flushed with pleasure.

"I am Huw of the Jomsvikings. I claim you, woman," he continued in a commanding tone that brooked no argument. "You will be my bedmate, now and for all time."

This can't be! Being claimed as the warrior's bedmate would mean leaving the Ironwood. Surely, the gods could not ask that of me.

Tangling his fingers in the hair at the nape of her neck, he drew her in to his hard frame. Astrid barely had time to gasp before his mouth descended, roughly claiming hers. His other hand stroked down her spine, trailing his finger between the cheeks of her ass, rimming the rosette that resided there, and cupped her cheeks, fondling and squeezing greedily.

What kind of vision is this? some part of Astrid's mind had time to wonder, before the stranger put both hands beneath her buttocks and lifted her up. Without thinking, she entwined her legs around his hips. The warrior growled with animal lust and drove into her, impaling her on his powerful cock. Astrid cried out and moaned at the same time, overwhelmed by the sensations running through her body.

By the gods, he's strong! Astrid thought in astonishment as he supported her in his arms. Rather than thrusting into her, he was rocking her body back and forth, effortlessly sliding her up and down the length of his shaft. She could not stop what was happening even if she wanted to...and she didn't want to. This growing feeling was exactly as Kasia had described it.

His grip was like iron. Astrid surrendered to the warrior, writhing in his arms, arching her back in sheer ecstasy. The stranger buried his face in her breasts, his beard rasping against her sensitive skin as he teased them with his tongue. When he took one of her tightened nipples between his teeth, Astrid could bear it no more, and her orgasm exploded, encompassing all of her senses.

The warrior was merciless, forcing her to ride his cock even as wave after wave of climaxes washed over her, rocking her body with their intensity. She wailed as she came again, a complete and total slave to his driving cock.

Astrid briefly recovered the ability to speak and

cried, “No more! Sacred Freyja, no more!”

“I. Claim. You!” he roared, emphasizing each word with a titanic thrust.

At the final word, he came, his cum flooding her sheath. Astrid was panting, her body shaking, her pussy pulsing along his length. She was barely conscious of him lowering her gently to the ground, withdrawing from her before standing over her, gazing down, the remnants of their coupling dripping from the end of his barely softened cock. Astrid fought to keep her eyes open. As she succumbed to exhaustion, she looked up a final time to memorize his face.

As the vision faded, he said, “Remember me, woman. You please me. I have claimed you, and thus you are mine.”

When she woke, it was morning. The fire had died, and she was lying on her blanket, wrapped in her cloak. *Was that my vision? What did it mean*? Kasia’s vision had been of a strong warrior as she used him to sire the child she now carried. Her vision had come true. Believing she needed to talk with her friend, Astrid gathered her things and returned to her village.

Chapter Two

"Come aboard, you misbegotten son of a herring! We've a tide to catch!" called the unmelodious voice of the shipmaster.

As it echoed in his ears, Huw, powerful warrior of an ancient tradition, shook his head and grinned.

"Rugen, you braying old goat," Huw called back. "I'm far from the last, and you know it."

On many ships, this exchange might have signaled a bare-knuckle fight. But Huw had a reputation as a man not to be trifled with, and the two were old friends.

"You're letting him talk to you like that?" asked Volund in disbelief, as he stood next to Rugen.

"Shut your mouth!" Rugen said quickly under his breath. "He doesn't mean anything by it, and he's a Jomsviking."

Volund blanched and quickly found something else to do. The Jomsvikings were legendary warriors and mercenaries, selling their swords to whoever was willing to pay. Huw pulled himself easily over the gunwale and onto the longship. He clapped the shipmaster on the shoulder.

"Well met, old friend," Huw said with feeling. "Who's that fellow who just skulked away?"

Rugen winced and answered in a lowered voice, "He's one of the crew and means no harm. He didn't know who you were, that's all."

Huw's chest shook with laughter. "As long as he stays out of my way, he'll come to no harm."

"How is it with you?" asked Rugen, knotting a line to the sail. "Strike me down if you don't look like a bit of a moon-calf."

Huw snorted. "Nothing really. My head's still just a bit fogged with dream-wisps. I met a woman..."

"A good dream, then!" Rugen chuckled.

"It was. By Odin, she was something—buxom and more responsive than any I've bedded. My need to possess her both during the dream and now is great. I'm just trying to recall her in more detail...it was important I think." Huw shook his head a third time.

"Aye, well, fate is fate," he said with a shrug before returning to the rigging. "If she's meant for you, you will find her again...this time in the real world. If not, you've still had more bed work than I've had in a month."

"I'm sorry to hear that, old friend. Who gave you the gift of prophecy?" laughed Huw.

***

Huw stood on the deck taking it all in—these jade-green days, where rock and pine climbed out of the deep-green water to form island upon island. Some were so small two seagulls were too many; some large enough to hold a single dwelling in comfort; and still others stretching back into the mist, filling the dark corners and shadows of the early evening. The longship, with its shallow draft, was made to travel here, slipping through the gaps and passages like an otter.

Huw joined Rugen at the rail. "How are the waters, Shipmaster?" he asked amiably.

Rugen smiled. "A fair wind and a following sea. As good as any sailor could wish for. How far will you be sailing with us, Huw?"

"I'll be stepping off when we reach the island of Gotland. The port of Visby, if you please."

"Ah." Rugen nodded. "Jomsburg business, then?" he asked, referring to the mighty fortress where the Jomsvikings made their home.

Huw shook his head. "Jomsburg's business is its own."

Rugen gestured to the tiller-man, sending him away and taking control of the ship's rudder. "But I'm am old and trusted friend."

No one else was near, and he looked at Huw and raised an eyebrow.

"Fine." Huw snorted as he sat against the gunwale near the ship's stern, facing forward so he could see if anyone approached. "I'm hunting a man, Ru," he said, tying his hair back to stop it from blowing into his face.

Rugen whistled softly. "Blood feud?" he asked.

Huw shook his head in denial. "Not exactly. He didn't kill anyone of my family. But he is—or was—a Jomsviking. He attacked a brother who was sleeping then fled into the night."

"He broke the code of your brotherhood?" asked Rugen in surprise.

Hugh nodded. "He raised his hand against a brother, without demanding a fair fight. He is an oathbreaker, and his life is forfeit. A vote was taken, and I was selected to do the deed."

An oathbreaker was rare among the Jomsvikings—a band of brothers who risked their lives for coin, and for one another, trusting each other to have their backs. Those who broke their oath were outcast, and such men did not live long.

"Why you?" inquired Rugen, curious.

Huw gave him a look, but he and Rugen had known each other for a long time, since before Huw had joined the Jomsvikings, and the sailor had his confidence.

"I volunteered," replied Huw. "The man he attacked was a friend. A good friend and he may yet die."

There was silence between them for a while.

Huw's mind went unbidden to the morning he had come upon Brynn's chambers. Brynn had looked as if he were sleeping, until his body had been disturbed, which had revealed that he had suffered a nearly lethal puncture. A silent and vicious strike. A coward's blow. Huw had swiftly searched through his friend's belongings and cursed. The *bengand* had been stolen.

The *bengand* was a powerful magical object. Only Huw and one other person had known it was in Brynn's possession. Huw had realized almost immediately who the culprit must be. Sure enough, Eirik had been nowhere to found within the Jomsburg.

"We will be at Visby within the week," Rugen said, breaking the silence and bringing Huw back to the here and now. "As long as these winds still hold, mind you."

“Fate is fate,” answered Huw.

Chapter Three

The next morning, Astrid and Kasia sat talking and laughing as they carded wool. The work was necessary—good wool meant warm clothes for the winter, and hopefully a surplus to sell—but it was not mentally taxing and gave the two of them time to talk.

"I tell you this, Astrid," she said as she continued to laugh, "there's many a witch in the Ironwood who would give her eye teeth for a vision like that. By the goddess Freyja, I haven't had a tumble myself since my last trip to Visby, and that was a lad more endowed than skilled!"

Astrid did not share her friend's amusement. "That was my *utiseta*, Kasia," she scowled. "My very first one. It's supposed to be a defining moment! But what did it mean? How do I interpret it? What am I supposed to do now?"

"Do it again. Maybe you can be lucky a second time."

"It's not funny, Kasia!" Astrid angrily picked a burr out of the wool on her lap.

Her friend stopped laughing and reached out to

stroke Astrid's hand.

"I'm sorry," said Kasia soothingly. "I don't mean to mock you. Truth to tell, I *am* a little bit jealous. You make it sound rapturous—a lovemaking for the ages. And the warrior you describe puts the sire of my child to shame...and that's saying something."

Despite herself, Astrid grinned. "He...it...was something. I never imagined anything like that even *existed*, much less that I would experience it." Her doubt returned. "I just wish I knew what it meant!"

"You could talk to one of the elders," suggested Kasia.

"In Conclave? With all the sisters gathered?" said Astrid, in horror. "I couldn't. It would be too embarrassing!"

"No, silly," laughed Kasia. "Of course not. I meant you should approach one the elders informally, and ask her what she thinks your vision means."

"That is sound advice, Kasia," said Astrid thoughtfully.

"Of course, it is. Now, tell me again about when he picked you up and..."

"Kasia!"

They both dissolved into giggles.

***

Later, Astrid made her way to the dwelling of Lady Brede, one of the elders who was always ready to talk with one of the younger witches. She had seen so much and was so willing to share all that she had experienced or to quiet the fears of others.

"Lady Brede?" said Astrid hesitantly, pulling back the heavy leather curtain to reveal the darkness therein.

"Come in, young one."

Astrid stepped into the room where Brede sat. It was dark, for the witch within needed no candle.

"Is that you, Astrid? Light a candle for yourself, and be welcome."

Astrid entered, using the taper she carried to light a tall candle in the wrought-iron holder near the middle of the room. A flickering circle of light expanded to reveal a woman with long gray hair who rested in a comfortable chair near her bed. She turned her face to the young witch, revealing features that were dignified, but kind.

Brede's eyes, however, were milky white. Rumor had it that she had sacrificed her eyesight to the Aesir gods, in exchange for inner vision of enormous power, and they had accepted her offering. Sacrifice for the sake of their fellow witches, especially to keep the

Ironwood strong, hidden, and safe, was a tradition that ran deep among the sisterhood.

The elderly witch smiled. “Sit down, child, and make yourself comfortable. I recommend the end of my bed. You come with questions.” It was a statement, not a question.

Astrid did as she’d been bid. “I do, Lady Brede. Last night was my first *utiseta*.”

“Ah, how delightful,” murmured Brede. “Beginnings are something special, something sacred. Nothing can replace them.”

“Lady Brede, my beginning has left me with many questions.”

Brede swept a hand, encouraging Astrid to go on. Flushing nervously, Astrid told the older witch about her vision. She was glad she didn’t have to meet her eyes. When she was done, there was a brief silence. Brede was nodding her head.

“That is a powerful vision, young one,” she said, finally.

“I just wish that I knew what it meant,” said Astrid earnestly.

“Well,” said Brede, “I think that it means great changes are coming for you, my dear.”

“What do you mean?”

"Sometimes," began Brede, "our visions come from inside of us. One thing can represent another. If that was the case here, a male figure could represent the shadow side of yourself, the most powerful forces that are at work inside you that you do not comprehend. But I do not think that is the case."

Astrid frowned. "Then what *do* you think it means, Lady Brede?"

The elder witch smiled, her face turned to Astrid, her sightless eyes seeming to bore into her. "I think that you are going to meet someone...a man...very soon. This warrior of your dream will change your life."

"He's real?" Astrid hesitated. "The man in my vision is *real*?"

"I would say that you should be open to the possibility of more new beginnings," said Brede simply.

Astrid took a deep breath, expelling it slowly. "Thank you, Lady Brede," she said respectfully. "This...this gives me much to think about."

She rose from the bed and impetuously hugged her.

"Please extinguish the candle on your way out," Brede reminded her. "No sense in wasting things."

Astrid murmured acknowledgement and blew the candle out, stepping from the darkness back into the light of the day, hesitating just outside the dwelling.

She could hear the old woman laughing softly as she whispered to herself, “Oh, young one...Fate has some surprises in store for you.”

Astrid’s mind reeled as she walked away, looking for her friend Kasia. *He is real*? *What can this mean? Am I to meet him?* Her body was sending her some clear signals about how it felt about such a prospect. *Was that...encounter a premonition of my future*?

Astrid was not a virgin. The Witches of the Ironwood understood the power of sexuality very well; they knew how to use it in their favor rather than be vulnerable to it. Still, nothing in her experience had ever come close to the raw power of her vision. In her vision, she had been absolutely helpless, bent to the strange warrior’s relentless will.

Her people had taught her how to use her sexuality, drawing power from it, even using it as a tool under certain circumstances. But what had happened in her vision...that was nothing over which she’d had any power. She had been the one who had been used, and the warrior had done the using. Never had she experienced anything that rivaled the raw sexuality of his use. The real problem was she couldn't escape the thrall of what had happened. It was as if he had cast a spell upon her...one she couldn't break and wasn't sure she wanted to. The fact was...she wanted more.

She should have been enraged by his treatment of her. Instead, she had been enthralled. His words had evoked something deep within her. A longing she had never known or dared to acknowledge. That's what was bothering her most—not just that it had happened or that it might be a portent of things to come, but that she couldn't say she wouldn't welcome it.

Astrid sighed and rubbed her temples. She could lie to others, but she couldn't lie to herself. She had been truly mastered—dominated and forced to submit. Even though it had only happened in her vision, she couldn't deny that she wanted it to happen again.

Kasia came running to meet her. "Astrid!" she called in an alarmed tone. "There you are!"

Knowing it was unlike Kasia to be anxious or fearful, she asked "What is it?"

"Terrible trouble is coming to the Ironwood," she said grimly as she steered her toward the Grove, the clearing at the heart of the Ironwood.

Astrid snorted in disbelief. "That can't be," Astrid said, allowing Kasia to lead her. "Our magic is still strong. We remain hidden from the world."

"But it can. The witch-ward started howling a little while ago. Then they went silent as if something had shut them off," replied Kasia.

"You can't simply shut them off..." Astrid began, having to concentrate in order to avoid tripping over her feet as Kasia quickened her pace and they joined other witches heading in the same direction.

"Can or can't doesn't matter right now," Kasia said firmly. "Something's happening, and we need to find out what it is."

They sped down the trail that led in a spiral toward the Grove, none of them tempted to stray from the well-worn path. From the time they were children they were taught that the Spiral and the Grove were the pulsing, mystical heart of the Ironwood. The magics that ran throughout were ancient and secret, and to stray from the trail was to be unmade by the eldritch powers within.

As Kasia and Astrid reached the clearing, they could see one of the elder witches drawing water from the sacred well, while two others prepared the scrying bowl. Many others were gathering around them anxiously, though not so close as to disturb what they were doing.

Water was poured into the bowl, and the witches breathed on the surface of the water to calm it. Astrid and Kasia struggled to see what the surface of the water revealed, but the crowd was too large and they had been among the last to arrive.

"So, it is true. The prophecy will come to pass unless we find a way to subvert it. A man, a warrior, will bring evil and ruin to the Ironwood," breathed one of the elders, a witch named Gunhilde.

"How is that possible? Surely, we can stop him. How could he silence the witch-ward?" demanded another.

Gunhilde looked more closely into the bowl, and paled as she shook her head in disbelief. "No," she whispered. "He carries with him a strong magic. He brings with him a *bengand*."

"A bone-wand!" several witches exclaimed in unison.

There were mutterings and whispers amongst the more senior members of their tribe.

"How could he possess such a thing? Where could it have come from?" asked one. "They were all lost, generations ago!"

Kasia and Astrid looked at each other in alarm. The Witches of the Ironwood had long ago woven many protections against the violence of men into their sacred forest. A *bengand* was part of an ancient magic that cut through witchcraft like a sword through cobwebs. They would be defenseless against the man who wielded it.

"What can we do?" asked an elder named Sigrid, in alarm. "Our magics will be as nothing, should this man wish us harm."

"He does wish us ill," came a voice from the rear of the clearing.

The witches turned to see blind Brede standing near the entrance to the Grove.

"Brede, my sister," gasped Gunhilde, "how did you...?"

"Please," smiled Brede, "my feet have walked the spiral path since you were a child." Her voice, though soft, carried through the clearing. "I tell you now, I have seen a vision...this man means to destroy us and our way of life."

There were gasps of shock and dismay. Brede's visions were never wrong.

"But," she continued, "the outcome is not certain. Though the magic he wields is powerful, we are not without our own. The goddesses have not turned their faces from us. One of our younger sisters has been shown a way that we might be saved from destruction."

A chill ran down Astrid's spine. *Surely not me?* She became cold…very, very cold.

Sightless or not, Brede turned her gaze to the young witch. "Astrid has been shown the champion who can defeat this ill-omened man and keep the Ironwood safe."

Beside her, Astrid heard Kasia's sharp intake of breath.

Brede beckoned her. "Come child…step forward."

The others moved aside, and with shaking steps, Astrid stood before Brede and the elder witches.

"I am here, Lady Brede," she said softly.

Brede reached forward and took Astrid's shoulder in a gentle but firm grasp.

"I charge you Astrid to leave the Ironwood. Go and find our champion. You will find him in Visby. He already seeks the one who means us harm. Guide his steps and remove this danger from our world."

"I…" began Astrid helplessly.

She felt lost, but then she heard Brede's voice in her mind. *Fear not, young witch. This is your fate, and the goddesses smile upon you.* Astrid straightened her shoulders and thrust her chin up, to look directly

Witch and Warrior

at Brede.

"I shall do this thing, Lady Brede. I will undertake this task and swear to see it through. I so swear by Freyja, Frigga, and all the Divine Ladies."

A murmur of approval passed through the Grove.

Brede smiled warmly. "I knew you would, sister. Prepare yourself for your journey. We will help you gather what you need. You will leave for Visby at first light tomorrow."

As the witches left the Grove, each one stopped to give Astrid an embrace and a blessing. Finally, only Kasia and Astrid were left standing in the clearing.

"Well," said Kasia, breaking the silence, "you wanted to know the meaning of your vision. Now you do."

Breaking the tension, Kasia laughed and rubbed her friend's shoulder. They began to walk along the spiral path.

"Kasia, don't you dare laugh. This is serious," blurted Astrid, torn between anger, fear and humor. "This is not what I was looking for! What must I do to keep our sisters safe? Are the goddesses going to demand that I surrender myself to this man as Lady Brede sacrificed her vision?"

"You might not have been looking for this, but fate

cares little for what we want. Fate is fickle and does as it chooses. It has a funny way of turning all of our plans upside down, and what else can we do but deal with it as best we can?"

Astrid shook her head. "When I woke up this morning, I never imagined a day such as this."

"No, you were far too involved reliving what it was like to have a very large co..."

"Kasia!"

Kasia held her gaze until both began laughing as they made their way up the spiral path.

Chapter Four

In his dream, Huw was walking. He was proceeding down a narrow trail, lined closely by fir trees. The trail twisted and curved, and he could not see its end. The foliage muffled sound, and as he walked quietly, he felt as if he were completely alone in the world.

I wonder what this means. What will happen when I wake?

He could see an opening ahead in the dense vegetation. The path widened to a clearing, and Huw stepped into a peaceful alpine meadow, a stream wound its way through. The sound of its passing was the only sound Huw could hear. In the center of the clearing stood a hall. Its thatched roof gleamed like gold.

"Well," said Huw, hitching his belt up, "I suppose my way seems pretty clear, then."

He felt no sense of urgency. The trail was soft on his feet, a gentle breeze blew through the grass, and the buzzing of bees rose to accompany the burble of the stream as he walked.

A man could find his ease here.

Huw had arrived at the hall itself. Its foundation was of stone, and there were steps carved into it. He slowly walked up the steps and stood on the verandah, which was made of the same thick stonework. He looked in marvel at the intricacy of the interweaving patterns worked into the stone then turned his gaze to the doors. Two doors, hanging heavy, with wrought-iron bands and hinges. Huw placed a hand on one, and, for all its weight, it moved smoothly inward.

"Hello?" he called out as he entered.

The hall was dark, save for two torches that burned at the far end. He could not see clearly but thought he saw some sort of dais.

"Hello?" he called again, and jumped, startled, as he felt a gentle but firm push at his ankle. Huw looked down to see a sizable cat weaving between his feet, purring. He chuckled, feeling a bit foolish. "Hello, mouser."

He reached down to scratch the cat between its ears.

"Leave him, Illvirki," called a low-and-sultry voice which was strange, yet oddly familiar, from the other end of the hall. "You may visit with our guest later, but for the moment he is mine."

"Who are you?" called Huw, trying to pierce the darkness, trying to see who had spoken. As he moved forward, he could see the torches framed not so much a dais or altar as a bed. "My name is Huw, and I seek shelter."

"Welcome, warrior. Even though you might call me stranger, we have met once before."

The hairs along the back of his neck stood on end.

"Dream-woman?" he whispered. Could it be the woman he'd met in the clearing—the one he'd fucked so decisively in his strange dream?

"Come forward," came the voice, low and sensual.

Huw gently nudged the very insistent cat away from his feet and stepped into the pool of light cast by the torches. He gasped. The bed that occupied the far end of the hall was massive, draped with furs and bedecked with pillows. It was high off the floor and reached by a small set of steps. But it was not the bed itself that made him gasp.

Instead, it was the naked woman reclining in the middle. Her hair fell in a cascading radiant auburn wave across her upper body. Hanging between her full breasts was a gleaming necklace of silver and amber that seemed to catch the light and shine like a star. She was propped against a pile of pillows and lay languorously stretched across the bed, a second cat purring in the crook of her elbow, its long tail curled around her taught nipple. She stroked the cat absently.

"Off you go, little Hugrakkur," the woman said, pushing the mildly complaining cat off the bed.

"Do you know who I am, Huw?"

How does she know my name? Did I tell her in the dream? Did she tell me hers? He searched his memory of the dream, still vivid and easily recalled. He was certain no names had been exchanged.

"Sur...Surely..." he stuttered finding it difficult to speak. His throat was dry and his mouth did not seem to be functioning properly. He tried again, more firmly. "Surely you must be Freyja?"

The woman smiled, spreading her legs to show him the glistening petals of her sex. She ran a single finger from slit to clit and crooked her finger at him. Huw swallowed. He needed to take control of this situation. No woman should be allowed to dominate an encounter with a warrior. Women, even one as beautiful as this, had their place, and it was not commanding a Jomsviking. They were meant for pleasure or to bear one's children. They did not entice a man and behave in such a manner.

"No, Huw," she said seductively, "although I work

Freyja's will in this matter. Thus, she has loaned us her hall for our dreaming."

"So, you are dreaming, too?" he asked before deciding he needed to take matters into his own hands and demanding, "It is you, isn't it? The woman I claimed? You are mine, but your name is unknown to me. Who *are* you?"

The woman rolled onto her knees, facing him. Her breasts dangled gloriously, barely covered by the auburn tresses of her hair as the necklace hung between them, twinkling and glittering in the light.

"My name is Astrid," she said, smiling directly at him.

Joy mingled with desire and rose up to cover him like the lapping of the sea.

"How is this happening?" Huw asked.

Astrid pushed some of her hair behind her ear. The cat bounded onto the bed and began rubbing its head against her hip. He felt a small stab of jealousy that the creature was touching what was his. The movement caught his eye as his gaze passed over the beautiful smooth curves of Astrid's bottom. A bottom that needed spanking before being taken for his pleasure. His cock had never been so hard. *It has to be a dream. Never has my cock hurt this much in waking life.*

"What do you think?" Astrid asked, amusement tinging her sultry voice.

Who does she think she is to mock me?

"I think everything in me is telling me this is real," Huw said honestly. "But I know that can't be so, for I know I am a passenger aboard a ship, sailing the ocean."

Astrid's taunting laugh was rich and low.

"But if that's true," he continued, "how can I possibly be here?"

"I think, Huw, that is a difficult question that deserves an answer. But the answer is not a simple one. I will try as best I can to make you understand." She straightened, holding out a long and graceful arm. "Come, sit, and I will try."

Again, she was forgetting her place. In real life, Huw would already have shown her by now, but this was a dreaming-world, and it made him cautious. He could smell her arousal, ripe and sweet. His cock throbbed, and he longed to sheathe it in her warmth—her mouth, her cunt or her ass. It didn't matter so long as he was buried up to his root. He took her outstretched hand and pulled her to him, running his hand down her back to cup and squeeze her full backside.

Astrid melted against him, rubbing her body against his as the cat had done before her. "Come, Huw. Let us get comfortable."

She turned back toward the bed.

"Huw!" she gently tsked. "I think you would be more comfortable without your boots...or other clothing."

"Hold, wench. I decide when I get naked."

"Of course," she teased him, running her hand down to cup his hardened staff. "It was simply an invitation."

She released his hand and moved away from him, crooking her finger at him once again as she climbed onto the bed and curled up amongst the pillows.

Huw found it difficult to swallow. *What sorcery is this?* This was not his world, where she would already be on her back. *I will bide my time. Let this woman play her games. She will be mine.*

He removed his boots then untied his belt. He pulled the tunic over his head and then stepped out of his leggings. He stood in his smallclothes, his cock tenting them. Astrid raised an eyebrow and, holding her gaze he dropped his drawers, now naked as she. Her gaze seemed riveted to his engorged member.

"I hope you see this as honest praise," he said.

His cock had never been harder, or larger.

Astrid laughed low in her throat. "Or perhaps it is an offering to Freyja."

She extended her hand. He smiled and carefully ascended the steps, crawling onto the bed, sitting next to the pillows where she lounged, where he could watch her and take the appropriate actions if needed. His cock was fully aroused, and he found his gaze drifted from the pebbled nipples to her denuded sex. He meant to part her labia and drive himself into her before much longer. But if she might have information about what was happening, he needed it. Huw focused on keeping his breathing regular and even.

"I suppose the first thing I should tell you is that you and I have been chosen by fate."

"We are all chosen by fate, whatever our wills may be," replied Huw, trying to ignore the lust that clawed at him, demanding he take what he knew was his...fate be damned.

"That's true," she said thoughtfully. "Sometimes, we are fortunate enough to see what threads that fate is weaving. I have seen that ours have been woven together. Fate has made you my champion. So, Huw, lie back," she whispered, crawling toward him on all fours and placing a hand on his shoulder to ease him back onto the bed when she reached his hip.

"What—" began Huw, stopping when Astrid smoothly swung her leg over his hips and lowered herself onto his aching shaft.

"Sweet goddess!" he cried out, despite himself.

Astrid shuddered deliciously, her sheath trembling along his length as she licked her lips and began to gyrate her hips, ever so slowly. Huw clutched at the bedclothes, trying to find some bit of control. He knew he should pull her from him and place her beneath him. But her cunt was warm and tight, and being inside her was utter ecstasy. His eyes rolled back in his head, and he thought he might pass out from the sheer pleasure of her ministrations.

The sensations and enjoyment soared as she rocked her hips back and forth more quickly. Huw ground his teeth in an effort to regain control.

"Come for me, Huw. Prove yourself my champion. Fill me with your seed!"

Without warning, Huw grasped her hips and pulled her from his cock, forcing her onto her belly before pulling her to her knees and landing a stinging blow to her glorious backside. If ever a woman needed a hard spanking and an even harder fucking, it was

Astrid. If fate had bound them together, she would need to learn her place and what displeasing her lord and master would earn her.

Grasping her by the waist, he ignored his rampaging cock and began to spank her. Astrid struggled and squirmed but could not avoid his landing blow after blow across her backside, infusing a rosy color where his hand connected with her flesh.

"Huw, no!" she cried.

"Astrid, yes!" he replied, spanking her with increased vigor, ignoring his rising frustration at not being deep within her, but that would change as soon as he'd ensured she knew who ruled between them.

Huw held her steady, moved behind her, and spread her legs apart as he fisted her hair at the nape of her neck, forcing her upper torso down. With an inarticulate bellow, he surged forward, driving his cock to the very depths of her pussy, delighting as she cried out and shuddered from the force and pleasure of his dominant possession.

He gripped her hips, to hold her as he pounded into her, thrusting his cock with the strength born of every muscle in his body. Astrid gasped, fueling his lust to an even greater frenzy. Reaching under her, he fondled her breasts, tugging her nipples. He plunged into her again and again until he succumbed to the primal urge to conquer and fuck the woman before him, with no thought other than slaking his desire.

Huw hammered her cunt, reveling in her response as she came for him repeatedly. Time seemed to have no meaning or place in the haze of his lust. He had no idea how much time had passed, lost in a never-ending cycle of feeling her clamp down on him in exquisite rapture as he drove into her repeatedly. Finally, he could stand it no longer as his balls drew up and he slammed into her, flooding her womb with his seed.

Astrid threw back her head and cried out, her hair flying in a maelstrom as her pussy clamped down on his cock, and he came again, once more unleashing a torrent of his cum into her yielding body. Suddenly, he heard a rushing in his ears as he collapsed on the bed, struggling for breath. His body shook and was covered in a sheen of perspiration.

Spent, Astrid recovered rolling over to sit up and stroke his chest and stomach, soothing him and helping to bring him back to reality.

"Well done, my champion," she purred. "I will see you soon."

Huw found he could no longer keep his eyes open or hold onto her as her vision began to dissipate like the fog on the morning tide. He tried to say something, but Astrid laid a finger to his lips.

"Hush now, warrior mine, and sleep," she whispered. "Your journey will begin when you wake."

Huw fell asleep to the sound of purring.

***

Huw stood at the rail, looking out over the coast of Gotland. He ran his hand over his beard and thought briefly of telling Rugen about his dream, dismissing the idea almost as quickly as it came. *Hard enough for me to believe, and I'm the one who had the bloody dream.*

"A champion," she had called him, going over the sequence of the dream.

He listened to the cries of gulls overhead as they approached the shore. *A champion of what? And for whom*?

"Astrid," he said to himself, savoring the sound of her name on his tongue.

Next time he planned for his tongue to savor more than her name. He wanted to taste her unique femininity, feast on her and make a meal of her. He shook his head, trying to clear the vision that occupied his mind. He had to remind himself that was all she had been. Both times when he had fucked her, it had not been on this plane of existence, and yet she stirred and satisfied him in a way no other ever had. Even putting the sex aside, something he was reluctant to do, she had been stunning, in every way he could imagine. He closed his eyes recalling in vivid detail her eyes, lips, and hair. He sighed as his imagination brought forth the feel of her sleek flanks and generous breasts and the feel of his cock breaching the petals of her sex as he had thrust into her again and again.

"For Odin's sake," Huw cursed himself. *Pull your mind out of her cunt. The pleasure of fucking her will have to wait until I put down my quarry*. Once Eirik was dead, he could pursue his quest to find and take Astrid to his bed in reality and on a permanent basis.

"Visby ahead," said Rugen, coming up behind him and clapping him on the shoulder. "Maybe an hour, and we'll be docked."

Forcing the memory from his mind, Huw said, "Best ready my weapons then."

Going below, he gathered his things and ensured his weapons were sharp and in good order. After they docked, he said his goodbyes to the shipmaster and a couple of others he knew. Huw disembarked and headed down the dock, striding confidently.

As the sailors watched him go then returned to

their unloading duties, he couldn't help but overhear them.

"I'll breathe a bit easier now," muttered one, checking the knots on a bale.

"How's that?" asked another.

"If a man has to kill, then so be it," the first sailor murmured, "but what kind of man seeks death every day? That's what a Jomsviking does. Death walks in their shadows."

"Be glad that's his fate and not yours, I reckon." His friend shrugged.

Huw continued on his way, secure in the knowledge of his skills, but also aware danger could lurk anywhere and everywhere. He had information Eirik was already here; and he might well be, but then again, he might not. The villain would know Jomsburg would send someone to kill him. Whether that meant Eirik would try to rely on speed and cunning and turn around to try and trap his pursuer, depended on the character of the man himself.

Eirik is a tricky bastard, thought Huw, sweeping his gaze from side to side as he walked. *He'll set a trap, like as not.*

Huw proceeded to take a leisurely walk around the streets of the town that lay within the city's walls. He stopped at various shops and stalls, sampling foods and touching various wares so he could be seen and word of his presence would be relayed back to Eirik if he was here. *Let's see if I can flush out any unsavory characters.* As far as he could tell, he had no takers.

In that case, time for a drink. The best news and gossip was usually to be had close to the docks, so Huw completed his circuit and ended up in the common room of The Sailor's Rest, or simply The Rest, as it was generally known.

Taking a mug of ale from the barkeep, Huw surveyed the patrons already drinking there. A mix of sailors and locals, they all seemed more preoccupied with minding their business than anything else. He reminded himself it was still early. The company would grow with the coming darkness, and tongues would wag as drink loosened them.

The barkeep ambled over to refill Huw's jack from a large clay pitcher. "Just come in on the tide, friend?" the older fellow asked, pouring.

"Aye." Huw nodded. Deciding to chance his luck, he murmured, "There's a man I'm seeking."

He laid a piece of hacksilver on the table. The barkeep's expression did not change as he swept the silver into his apron. "There are many who pass through here on their way to somewhere else," he murmured.

"This one you would remember—big fellow, ill-tempered, bushy black moustache. Usually goes by the name of Eirik. He'll be looking to hire men, if I'm not mistaken."

The barkeep set the pitcher down, wiped his hands on his apron, and said softly, "A man like you're describing will be here as the sun goes down, if he keeps to his habits of the last week."

Huw nodded.

"And he won't be alone," the barkeep added as he turned and walked back toward the kitchen.

Huw gave it some thought as he savored his ale. The common room wasn't large enough to provide him with a shadowy corner to sink into as darkness fell. There was, however, a second-floor balcony containing a couple of tables. As long as there was no illumination, that might do the trick when the sun went down.

He stood and went to the bar, ordered a bowl of hot stew, and asked that it be taken to him at a table on the second floor, emphasizing he wanted a quiet spot. Huw slid another piece of hacksilver quietly across the bar to make sure the barkeep understood. The man nodded and made the silver disappear.

Time passed; Huw drank slowly. As he hoped, the afternoon crowd was replaced by the evening crowd, none of whom noticed the Jomsviking quietly observing them from the darkened balcony above. The sounds of laughter grew louder as the drink began to flow, and there were cheers as a local skald tuned his harp in preparation for a performance.

The cheers turned to a roar of welcome as Eirik strode through the door. As the patrons had hoped, the big man turned to the barkeep and said loudly, "A round for the company, good man, and set it against my tally!"

Huw's eyes narrowed as he assessed the situation. Eirik was indeed not alone. He was flanked by two unsavory but capable-looking fellows who appeared ready and willing to get their hands dirty with a little knife-work.

This could get awkward. Fighting three men at once means a dagger in my back, if I'm not careful.

His strategy and plans were interrupted and quickly refined by the sight of the barkeep talking quietly to Eirik as he passed out cups of ale. Huw watched with alarm as Eirik's shoulders stiffened. *Trollshit. The barman has sold me out. I guess Eirik is a bigger spender than me.*

He reassessed his options. His position still gave them a slight advantage...higher ground always did. If he could trap and engage them on the staircase, he could deal with them one at a time.

Huw watched as Eirik conferred with his companions. One of them moved to stand near the door, and the other next to a stout timber post he could easily climb to reach the second-floor balcony and prevent Huw from engaging them one at a time on the stairs.

Worse and worse. Eirik is actually playing it pretty smart. Who would have thought it?

"When the game is rigged, switch the pieces," he muttered, and tipped his now-cold stew over the balcony, straight onto the heads of the patrons below.

In the roaring chaos that followed, and before anyone could figure out what had happened, Huw cleared the balcony railing with a nimble hop, aiming for the table below him. Even as he landed, he bent deeply at the knees, exploding into a leap toward the door.

Completely caught off guard, Eirik's henchman was still reaching for his dagger when Huw's fist thundered into the side of his head, clouting him directly on the temple. The man went down like a poled ox, and, before anyone else could react, Huw was out the door and headed into the night, the echoes of Eirik's roar of anger and frustration receding into the distance.

Chapter Five

Astrid looked at the elder witches, trying to hide her nervousness.

"I've, ah, never traveled this way before," she ventured, disliking the timidity in her voice.

Gunhilde clucked her tongue. "Do not be afraid, young sister," she reproved. "Many have forgotten the art of sending, but not we of the Ironwood. Our sisterhood runs back beyond the memories of men."

"You'll be fine," said Sigrid, more reassuringly. "We've done this many times."

"It's just that I've never seen anyone do it," persisted Astrid.

"Rarely do we have need," explained Sigrid patiently. "We see a long way down the road, are surprised by little, and plan well. But now, distressingly, we find ourselves pressed for time."

"Stop complaining," laughed Kasia. "You've never been a timid mouse. What an adventure you are about to have...and think of what you'll learn. I'm as jealous as the cat that missed the cream."

"If you're so jealous, you do it," Astrid shot back

without any real rancor.

Kasia rubbed her belly. “Unfortunately, fate saw that I would be unable to take your place. I cannot risk the child I carry. Besides, it’s not my pussy that’s tuned to that fellow’s cock.”

Laughter filled the room as the elder witches shook their heads.

Gunhilde raised her hands, quieting them down. “All right,” she said, “Sigrid and I will begin the song of traveling. For a brief time, sister, you will be walking between worlds. Follow the path the song lays out for you, and do not leave it. Step through the door the song opens, and do not linger.”

Astrid nodded.

Kasia squeezed her hand. “Good luck,” said her friend.

Astrid gave her a quick squeeze back then bowed her head and clasped her hands together. Gunhilde began the chant, murmuring in a low tone. Astrid focused on breathing slowly. Sigrid joined in at a higher pitch, and Astrid felt the hair on the back of her neck rise. The chanting became more intense, and the voices of the two elder witches rose and fell, weaving between each other until you could no longer follow who was chanting what. There was a shimmering, and

Astrid raised her head.

It looked as if she was standing amidst the very stars, against a background of the darkest void she could ever imagine. Panicked, she briefly looked down and was overcome by vertigo and the terrible feeling that she was going to tumble into the abyss and fall forever.

"You will not fall, young sister." Sigrid's voice, warm and reassuring. "Simply walk the path."

Astrid could suddenly see a path before her, made of little lights strewn like flower petals. She began to walk and felt her perspective shift. It was as if each small step took her from one world to another. It was glorious. Strength surged within her and all around her. The feeling was intoxicating, and she had never felt more powerful in her life.

Even so, Astrid was relieved when a door appeared. If she stayed in this place between worlds too long, she would become mesmerized and never want to leave. She carefully stepped through the door...and found herself ankle deep in a small running stream, in a forest she didn't recognize. Cursing under her breath, she moved to dry ground and tried to shake the water out of her shoes.

Deciding that she was better off with dirty feet

that were dry, she took off her shoes and stockings, tying the laces of her shoes together and hanging them from her belt. Wringing out her stockings, Astrid looked around and tried to make sense of where she was.

"Oi! Mind yourself, why don't you?" came an indignant cry from somewhere near her feet.

Surprised, Astrid looked down to see one of the *landvettir*, a tiny gnomelike fellow, angrily shaking water from his hat. She realized that she had been the unintended cause of his soaking.

"I'm very sorry," said Astrid contritely, crouching down. "I didn't see you there."

"Well, you wouldn't, would you?" groused the gnome. "Popping out of nowhere into my stream, ruining my fishing. I'm blessed if I know where my rod's gone..."

The little creature's indignation was so unintentionally comic that Astrid had to cover her mouth briefly. The gnome was too occupied with the dampened state of his clothing to notice.

"May I help you to dry off, sir?" she inquired. Her training had taught her that it was unwise to earn the enmity of the *landvettir*.

"Seems only fair," said the gnome grudgingly, and,

to her astonishment, he quickly removed all his clothing and stood stark naked in front of her. "Come on, then," he grumbled, grabbing a section of her skirt and vigorously toweling himself off.

"Ah..." Astrid was momentarily at a loss for words.

The gnome did not seem to notice. After he toweled himself off, he wrung out each item of tiny clothing thoroughly before putting it on again. Astrid just watched in amazed, and slightly horrified, fascination. The *landvettir* had the most misshapen penis she'd ever seen...not that she had made a study of men's cocks, but this was decidedly odd. It looked to be longer than one might imagine, but not of great girth, and twisted, with raised spirals starting at the base of his phallus and wrapping around its entire length.

"Well," said the gnome, patting himself down, "that's about as good as I can do until I get my bum in front of a fire. Now, who are you, missy, and what in the name of Midgard are you doing popping into my stream?"

As bemused as she was, Astrid was well aware of the correct protocol amongst the *landvettir*. "Before I give you my name, you have the advantage of me, good sir."

The gnome nodded approvingly. “So, I do. My name is Magnus. Magnus the Great, I am known amongst my people.”

Astrid coughed. Magnus looked at her suspiciously for a moment, but she kept her expression composed.

“My name is Astrid,” she replied. “I come from the Witches of the Ironwood.”

The gnome nodded. “That explains how you ended up going sploosh right in front of me. Well, good fortune to you. I’m off to make a fire before I catch my death of cold.”

“Wait!” Astrid protested. Magnus paused. “I’m, ah...I’m a first-time traveler. Can you point me in the right direction for Visby?”

Magnus jerked a thumb westward. “Two miles as the crow flies, maybe two and a half as the gnome runs. Go straight west, and you’ll hit the road.”

The gnome suddenly let forth with an enormous sneeze. “You see? Be on your way, witch, and no more questions! I’m off to warm up before I catch my death!”

Magnus tromped off into the forest, away from the stream.

“Fare thee well, Magnus,” Astrid called after him.

Magnus waved a hand dismissively, muttering irritably under his breath, something about his fishing rod. She hoped.

"Right," said Astrid to herself, and set out due west.

As Magnus had said, it wasn't long before she reached the road, which was closer to a wide trail with deep wagon ruts. The forest arched up on either side of it, and the branches of the trees crossed over it, giving only occasional glimpses of the sky.

Astrid's sense of caution prickled. Should she take the road, or would she be better keeping herself hidden in the forest with the road in sight? She was not helpless by any means, but her magic would be useless if she ran into the man who had the *bengand*. Witch magic was as nothing against someone wielding a bone-wand.

Still. Her feet were sore, and her shoes and stockings had yet to dry. The road would be easier than the prickly underbrush of the forest.

"Besides," she told herself crossly, "Witches of the Ironwood have a fearsome reputation, and rightly so. What's the point if we have to walk in fear?"

Astrid had just made up her mind to step out of the forest and onto the road when the sounds of a ferocious tumult echoed, down the road and coming closer.

On the other hand, we're not idiots. She took a position behind a tree where she could be concealed but still observe what was happening.

From around a bend in the road came three men, running as fast as they were able. Their speed was hindered by the fact they kept looking behind them. All three were warriors by their dress and appearance, and Astrid wondered what could make them run in such fear.

Her question was answered as a man burst from the trees on the other side of the road from where she was hiding. The man wasted no words on the fleeing warriors, hurling a spear that caught one warrior high in his chest. The warrior catapulted backward like he'd been slapped by a giant. The stranger did not pause, pulled a sword from his belt and opened the throat of the second warrior with a wicked backhand slash.

Astrid was in shock. Not because of the violence, which was terrible enough, but because the stranger was the man of her visions.

"*Huw!*" she cried out involuntarily.

"Astrid?" he said, seemingly so surprised at the sound of her voice he lowered his blade, almost losing his head as the final warrior swung an axe at him in a blow that could have easily been lethal.

Astrid screamed, but Huw managed to recover, leaning so far back at the last moment that he overbalanced and had to go to one knee. With a desperate shout, the other warrior rushed forward to press his advantage, axe at the ready.

Even as Huw prepared to lunge at him, the warrior screamed and fell. Coils of green fire wrapped around his head and neck, sizzling as they burned. Shuddering, Astrid ceased chanting as the warrior made one last desperate convulsion and died... the first time Astrid had taken a human life.

She had no time to think about the implications of her actions as she was confronted by a furious Huw. "Foolish girl! Do you have any idea how close you came to getting yourself killed?"

"Getting myself killed?" she railed. "I saved..."

"You saved nothing that would have needed saving if you hadn't popped up out of nowhere and called my name in the middle of my ambush! I've a good mind to put you over my knee right now and spank some sense into you!"

Heat rising in her cheeks, Astrid shouted back, "Go ahead and try it! Or did you not see what happened to the man I saved you from?"

"You put yourself in danger, against my orders, and then threaten me with witchfire? You'd best be careful, girl. You're this close to receiving another sore bottom!"

"Stop calling me girl! You'll back away if you know what's good for you!" Astrid replied hotly, raising her hands. She wasn't actually going to cast deadly witchfire at him, but he needed to back off and show some respect.

"I'll call you what I choose, *girl* and you will learn to answer," snarled Huw. He seized Astrid and threw her over his shoulder then carried her into the forest.

Shrieking with anger, Astrid attempted to cast a spell in earnest, but it slid off him like water off a duck.

Huw laughed grimly. "Foolish girl. Do you not know that we of the Jomsburg have protections against witchfire?"

Finding a log, he sat down, pulled her over his lap, trapping her legs between his. Astrid found herself staring at the ground, his cock quickly becoming engorged and throbbing beneath her.

"Unhand me, you barbarous oaf!" she demanded.

"Barbarous oaf? Hardly. Lord and master."

His hand came down in a crashing arc on her

backside. He walloped her several times as she yelped, and tried to lift herself up off his lap. Strong as she was, she couldn't get away from him. It was if she was struggling against stone. Again, and again, his hand came down on her rump. Astrid struggled and squirmed.

"You will be still and accept my discipline," warned Huw, "or this skirt will come up and I'll take my hand to your bare bottom."

"You wouldn't dare," seethed Astrid.

"Wrong answer, girl." Huw pulled up her skirt and tucked it into her belt. He placed his hand on her heated buttocks. "Last chance," he warned. "Time to apologize, or it'll be the worse for you."

"I've done *nothing* to apologize for!"

"That's the second wrong answer."

Huw began spanking her with decidedly more enthusiasm, his cock responding by quickly becoming engorged and ready to fuck. He sniffed the air and smiled. Astrid's arousal was quickly replacing her ill temper—or at least taking a place beside it. He was as hard as an iceberg and hot as a mineral spring. Her buttocks bounced delightfully under his hand, and all the intimacies that Huw had shared with Astrid in their dreams came to the forefront of his mind. His desire rose with every swat. He began landing each blow, allowing his hand to lie against her flesh to hold in the heat before giving it a good squeeze.

For Astrid, what had started as an infuriating display of dominance was rapidly becoming something inescapable, a dance of desire and pain, to which she was beginning to lose herself. His grip was like iron, and despite all her struggles, she was unable to change what was happening to her by even the slightest degree. She was being spanked, and spanked thoroughly, and there was not a single thing she could do about it.

Even more infuriating was her body's response to his punishment. Past the pain she felt all across her rapidly swelling bottom, was the growing tingle of sensation rushing to her feminine parts and spreading outward. *How can my body find this arousing*? she thought, feeling betrayed by her own body. She hoped and prayed he didn't notice the evidence of her arousal beginning to pool at the entrance to her feminine core.

As Huw continued to make her cheeks bounce, methodically and enthusiastically turning them hot and swollen, Astrid's tears of frustration and anger turned into deeper sobs.

"Please stop," she keened. "Please!"

Huw lightened the severity of his punishment but did not stop. "Have you learned your lesson?" he asked, sternly.

"Yes," Astrid sobbed.

Huw rested his hand on her warmed bottom. "And what is that lesson?" he asked, a bit more gently.

"Not to come between a warrior and his foe."

"True," he agreed, before bringing his hand down again, right on her sit spots. "And?"

"Not to distract a warrior when his life is at stake," Astrid said tearfully.

"Also true, girl," crooned Huw, his voice softening as he began to rub gently and soothingly across her bottom. "It was my life at risk. But remember, it was also yours. Had those men taken my life, your fate would not have been much better. I would not have you harmed."

"What do you call what you just did?" wailed Astrid.

Huw chuckled. "I'd call that a lesson well needed and hopefully well learned. If it is needed again, it will be sword strap and not my hand that instructs you."

He helped her to her feet before standing. Huw

was taller than her by at least a head, but Astrid glared up at him and wiped the tears from her face.

"Bully," she seethed.

"If you say so, girl," he chuckled.

His easy superiority infuriated Astrid. *Has this lout no idea of who I am*? Furious, she snaked her hand out to slap his face.

Catching her wrist easily, he warned, "Careful now, girl."

Further enraged by his handling of her, Astrid brought the other hand up as well. This, too, he caught before it could do any damage.

"That is not the way to make me believe you have learned your lesson, but as it is clear you have not been spanked before, I will teach you another way your lord and master can bring the lesson home."

He fisted her mane and pressed on her shoulders, forcing her to his knees in front of him. He opened his trousers allowing his cock to spring free. This was the first time she had been confronted by it in the flesh, and it was every bit as imposing as in her visions. He clutched her jaw between his fingers, forcing her mouth open.

"You know what I want?"

She nodded.

"Do you know what I'll do to you if I so much as feel your sharp little teeth on my staff?"

She nodded again. Every Witch of the Ironwood was taught to use her mouth to bring a man to full erection and even to completion. Huw stroked her jawline lustfully and pressed his cock against her lips and past her teeth, groaning as it slid along her tongue.

Astrid hesitated for a moment. His cock was enormous, long and thick and pulsed within her mouth. She looked at the part that wasn't yet engulfed by her lips. She extended her tongue, licking the underside as she tried to draw back. Huw stilled her head and pushed forward. He groaned and she felt her pussy tremble in response.

She had never felt this kind of arousal before. Her ass was on fire, her mouth was filled with his engorged cock, and her pussy threatened to leak its sacred fluid. Her body hummed with a kind of erotic energy and she understood why her people revered sex magic and its power.

"Good girl," he praised, pushing himself deeper to touch the back of her throat.

She took several inches in one long stroke over which she had no control. Huw was in charge, impaling her mouth on his staff. Her lips stretched to accommodate his thick, pulsing flesh. The flutter in her belly expanded and took flight as she swirled her tongue around him, causing him to groan. She closed her mouth around him and sucked deeply.

"Look at me," he growled, fisting her hair and tugging, lighting up her scalp.

Her eyes locked with his as he stared at her with masculine intensity. He released her hair, grasping her head in both hands, keeping her focused and under his control. Huw surged forward, forcing her to take his cock deep and swallow. Her lust fed off his with every surge of his rod between her lips.

Huw groaned again and began pumping hard, arching his back to force her to take him deeper. Astrid didn't think she could take more, but swallowed and took him far deeper than she'd ever thought possible.

"Gods," he hissed as his cum shot across her tongue and down her throat.

She'd never swallowed a man's seed before. Witches of the Ironwood always made them spend themselves on the ground or into a bowl to be used in potions. But there was no denying him; her acceptance of his treatment seemed to trigger his response. He continued to spill himself down her gullet, throbbing and twitching as he did so until his balls were emptied and her belly was full.

Huw pulled her from her knees and kissed her passionately, their lips and tongues meeting for the first time in a passionate embrace. Huw gripped her about the waist and hauled her into his body. Her arms snaked around Huw's neck to mold her mouth to his. Their lips connected in a fevered kiss, each of them driving their tongue into the other's mouth, claiming the other in a lustful frenzy.

He released her for a brief moment, separating them and giving him the time and opportunity to strip her of her skirt and blouse. She pushed his trousers down past his muscled buttocks. Then, with a mighty roar, Huw seized Astrid by her red-and-swollen buttocks, and lifted her up into the air.

For a moment she was mesmerized by his incredible strength–*just like in my vision*–before the head of his rigid staff, parted her nether lips, poised at her entrance to her core.

"Yes," she hissed into his ear, biting the lobe, "do it!"

With roar of pure animal lust, he did just that. Astrid cried out, both with the suddenness of his thrust and the all-consuming sensation of being filled completely.

In Huw's hands, Astrid seemed to weigh nothing more than a feather as he held her, driving into her again and again. The power of his claiming sent Astrid's sensations over the top, and she arched back in his arms as the first orgasm took her. She momentarily lost all sense of where she was, afraid she would pass out, but through it all was the shattering, glorious, inexorable driving of Huw's shaft, keeping her simultaneously rooted to the spot and lost to climax upon climax.

From being arched backward, held only by his iron grasp, Astrid clenched her muscles and pulled herself up to entwine her arms around his neck. Even as he slid her up and down the length of his cock, she gasped and dug her nails deeply into him. Huw seemed neither to notice nor to care, increasing the pace and intensity as he drove toward his own climax.

Astrid tried desperately to hang on to him, still trying to gain some sense of control, but, as his cock swelled and prepared for a second and final release, her own body spasmed beyond any restraint, and once again she arched back, impaled by his cock, gripped in his arms, her pussy pulsing along the length of his staff as he released a torrent of creamy essence deep inside her.

Huw stood there, Astrid in his arms, as the sounds of the forest gradually returned to their ears, time unfroze, and they slowly returned to reality. Astrid leaned forward to bury her head in his broad, powerful chest. He turned his head to rest his cheek against her hair, taking in the scent of her.

Astrid murmured, "I thought it was a vision...a dream. But it's real. *You're* real."

"You've haunted my dreams, girl. Like nothing ever has. And now you're here, in my arms," replied Huw.

Gently, he lifted her from his cock, withdrew from her and softly returning her to her feet. Her legs were shaky and weak, like a newborn fawn's. Huw pulled his trousers up, handed Astrid her clothing and allowing her to get dressed. The dreamlike quality of their coupling remained.

She reached forward and took his hand, wanting to maintain the sense of physical contact even as the glow from their frenzied lovemaking began to recede. He led her to the log, sat down, and pulled her into his lap. Astrid winced as her bottom made contact with his hard thighs, but sitting on him was less painful than the log. His hand had been like stone, or wood.

"You spanked me," she said, half in remembered outrage, half in wonder.

"I did," came Huw's frank reply. "And I will spank you again if you endanger yourself or disobey me." He chuckled. "You seemed pretty angry at first, but that was quickly replaced by arousal."

Astrid shook her head, wanting to negate his words, but they were true.

"Huw," she said, savoring the sound of the man's name in her mouth. "Huw, what is going on here? I see you in my visions. The elders of my people tell me our destinies are intertwined, that we have a purpose..."

"Fates intertwined, is it?" said Huw speculatively. "Perhaps. I know I have claimed you, but I don't know that I like being part of some witch scheme."

Astrid recoiled at the venom in his voice as he said the word *witch*.

"What is this anger in your voice when you speak of my Sisters of the Ironwood?" she asked, her temper beginning to rise.

"I'm Jomsviking," he said flatly. "A brotherhood forged in courage and fighting skill. We have neither time nor trust for the snares of witchfolk."

Astrid stood up, insulted. "But you're fine sticking

your cock in one, aren't you?"

"It's not that simple, woman," Huw said, standing. "You are mine regardless of what the elders of your sisterhood say. Nothing will change that. I have claimed you, and will fight any man who disputes my claim. And that wasn't what just happened, and you know it," he said sharply.

"Really?" Astrid snapped. "We're given visions from the gods, brought together in this forest, *make those visions a reality*, and it's nothing more than the 'snares of witchfolk'? You ignorant bastard!"

Huw's face darkened. "You mind your tongue, girl," he warned.

"Or what?" Astrid challenged him. "I'll go over your knee again?"

"Something like that, yes."

"Not bloody likely," retorted Astrid, taking a step back to give herself space.

"You may be protected against witchfire, but you're not untouchable."

"Really?" Huw stepped forward, eyes glinting with anger. "Come and touch me, then," he taunted.

"You asked for it," replied Astrid, snapping her fingers.

In that very instant, Huw's vision exploded into a series of bright lights and colors, whirling at speeds so great that he was seized with a sense of vertigo. Blinded and unbalanced, he reached out for a tree to steady himself.

By the time his sight cleared and the dizziness faded, Astrid was gone.

Spear and spindle, Huw, you're an idiot.

Chapter Six

Astrid seethed with fury as she ran through the forest, cursing Huw's name.

"Big-muscled, tiny-minded, cloth-eared beet!" she swore as she moved swiftly through the trees.

"The *nerve* of the man! 'Snares of witchfolk,' is it? Pick me up and have at me without so much as an if you please?"

Astrid stopped, trying to resolutely ignore and still the shudders of remembered pleasure that came with the memories of their coupling. If anything, they made her even angrier. She stamped her foot in vexation.

"Oi!" came the aggrieved cry of a familiar voice at her feet. "I don't go trampling on your house, do I?"

Astrid closed her eyes. *Of course, that's where I stepped.* "I'm sorry, Magnus," she sighed.

"That's Magnus the Great, to you! What did I ever do to you or yours, that you torment me so?"

Magnus was clearly still underground; she could hear his voice, but he could not be seen anywhere.

"Forgive me, good sir. My mind was on another things. It was purely accidental," said Astrid contritely.

"What in the Nine Worlds are you even looking for in my forest, tallpockets?" demanded Magnus' voice.

Astrid sighed. "I was seeking a man."

He chuckled a bit malevolently. "Certainly, looked to me like you found one. You're a bit of a wanton thing, aren't you?"

"You were *watching* me?"

"Can't blame a gnome. Forest gets a bit boring sometimes," came the amused answer.

"Sacred Freyja!" shouted Astrid, stamping her foot again without thinking.

"No need to bring my house down around my ears!" cried Magnus. "So, you sought a man, you found a man...*ahem*...so what are still doing here, disturbing the architecture?"

Astrid stood still. She really didn't have an answer. She had done what she had been supposed to do, and now, well, that was a mess she had left behind. Her beloved Ironwood still faced a threat, though—the dark stranger with the bone-wand, who meant to bring ruin to her home. She had to do *something.*

"Visby," she decided. "I'm going to Visby."

"Back to the road, you go, and turn west. Like I told you before. Off you go, then," said Magnus encouragingly. "Don't let the door hit your ass on the way out."

"Forests don't have doors," Astrid tossed back as she made her way back to the road.

"Shows what you know," Magnus shot back.

***

"Arrogant, presumptuous, evil-minded witch!" muttered Huw angrily as he stomped through the forest. "I'll teach you to seduce me with your womanly wiles and entangle me in your intrigues."

Huw resolutely ignored the itching of his palm as he thought about what he would do when he caught up with Astrid. She'd be lucky if it was his hand and not his belt. Harder to disregard was the stiffness of his cock, which had turned rock hard at the memory of his encounter with her. Coupling with her had been everything his dreams had promised, brought gloriously to life. How she had squirmed under the hand of his discipline. How she had screamed while her pussy was pummeled by his cock. The sheer world-obliterating glory when they had climaxed simultaneously.

Huw shook his head. Practically as soon as they had finished, she had plans. *Plans of the witch-women.* The sagas were full of the snares of the Witches of the Ironwood, and woe betide any man who found himself subject to one of their cunning schemes. In the rough and tumble halls of Jomsburg, they had a name for any of their warriors who seemed to have fallen under the spell of a woman: Witch-whipped.

It was *not* considered a desirable name.

On the other hand, there had been the dreams. Surely, they meant something, and a wise man did not lightly toss away the prophecies of the gods. Huw came to a halt, thinking. Really, there was only one path from here. He had to find Astrid again. He had claimed her, and she would be his. She would learn to obey and submit and, when she didn't, would find herself over his knee followed by the judicious use of his cock in one of her pleasure holes. He would teach her a lesson about using her magic against him. He would not be witch-whipped, literally or even figuratively. No, his witch would find her bottom whipped when she tried to use her magic to escape her proper place.

"Right," said Huw, gritting his teeth, as he set about finding and picking up Astrid's trail through the forest.

***

Astrid let her anger carry her along the road to Visby. She didn't even notice any sense of fatigue until the sun was high in the sky. She had covered a great deal of territory, been spanked and fucked thoroughly. But the smoke trails twisting into the sky heralded a large town. It had to be Visby. She pressed on.

She paused and stepped off the road long enough to find a private spot to pull on her now dry stockings and shoes. She tried to sort out her hair and general appearance and resolutely ignored the heat and soreness that still radiated from her bottom and the place between her thighs. Huw had an enormous staff and had used her hard.

Taking a break from her angry strides and furious thoughts about Huw, Astrid considered her position. Her instructions from her elders had been clear: find their champion, bend him to the will of the Ironwood, use him to eliminate the threat of the dark stranger with the *bengand* then send him on his way. It sounded so straightforward, when you put it like that. But she wasn't sure if Huw was a warrior who would be so easily discarded.

Well, she had found their champion. After that it had all gone amiss. She'd tried bending him to her will and ended up with a spanked bottom and well fucked pussy. The question was now...what to do? She certainly wasn't going back to that arrogant, overbearing...*okay, pause. You've been down that road all morning, Astrid.*

Right. The main threat was the wand-wielding man, who bore ill intentions toward the Ironwood. If that musclebound son of a *rassragr* wouldn't help her, then it was up to her to take the fellow down and take the bone-wand into the safe custody of her sisters.

Straightening her clothing, Astrid walked into Visby.

The town was familiar to her, as it was the main point of contact between the Ironwood and the outside world. Even so, there were buildings she didn't recognize, and new farmsteads outside the town. Visby was a bustling place, vibrant and constantly growing and changing.

Still, Astrid quickly picked out one homestead that she recognized, and she walked through the gate and into the yard. In front of the door was a young woman, weaving reeds to form a basket. The woman looked up at Astrid and smiled warmly, putting her weaving down and running over to embrace her.

"Astrid, my dear! How are you? It has been too long." The woman's smile was genuine and bright.

"Ignetha, my dear friend," returned Astrid warmly. "It has indeed been too long. It's delightful to see you."

"Come and sit," urged Ignetha, stepping into the house briefly before returning with bread and water, which Astrid took gladly, as she was ravenous. Ignetha waited politely for her friend to finish eating before asking her questions.

"So, what brings you here, Astrid? It's out of season for one of your usual visits. How is Kasia? Word on the wind is that she is with child. Who is the father? Does she know if it will be a boy or a girl?"

Astrid grinned at the stream of questions from her friend. Ignetha had been a loyal ally of the Ironwood Witches here in Visby, and had always provided visiting witches with food and shelter, even during those times when the opinions of Visby's leaders had been turned against the Ironwood.

"My word, Ignetha, you must be starved for news to have such curiosity! Things must be terribly dull here in town."

"You might think so, but you'd be wrong," said Ignetha, her eyes shining. "Only last night, there was a huge to-do at The Rest. Not just the usual brawl between sailors, mind you—a full on fight! Daggers out, jumping over balconies, chases into the night, true Viking stuff."

Astrid had a sinking feeling but tried to keep her face neutral. “Any idea who was fighting?”

“A couple of real warriors!” replied Ignetha breathlessly. “One was Eirik Blackmane, who has a dark reputation around Visby. He’s been gathering brigands to his side for a week or more, for some ill-favored task. And the other no one seems to know, except that he’s a Jomsviking, fresh from Jomsburg itself, apparently on some mission of vengeance against Eirik! Some are even saying it’s a blood-feud!”

Astrid sipped at her water. “So, what happened?” she encouraged her friend.

“No one seems to have a clear tale of it, but apparently the Jomsviking was waiting for Eirik. Eirik wasn’t alone, though—he never is, nowadays—and set his men on his enemy, trying to trap him. Apparently, this fellow jumped off the second-floor balcony, cracked one fellow’s head, knocked out another, and was off into the night before anyone could say a word! Not only that”—Ignetha leaned forward— “but Eirik sent men off into the night to find the Jomsviking, and they haven’t returned!”

“So, this Eirik wasn’t with them? Who is he anyway? What is known of him?” Astrid needed to know more.

Ignetha shook her head. "Not much other than one you keep a boat-length from. He's kin to the Skraelings."

Astrid almost dropped her cup. "Freyja preserve us," she muttered.

The Skraelings were a loose collection of families who held power in the bleak lands of the far north. A cold and cruel people, they were notorious for their vengeful natures. They never forgot an insult. Their only redeeming feature was that they hated each other almost as much as they hated everyone else, and generally spent their energy on internal squabbles.

"When Skraelings break bread, let the world dread," said Ignetha sorrowfully, quoting an old saying. "If they've stopped fighting each other long enough to have an eye on Visby..."

"Why don't they toss him out, then, if the city fathers are so concerned about him?" asked Astrid.

"They don't want to wake his anger," replied Ignetha. "They hope that he's gathering outlaws and raiders for something outside the city, and that his shadow will pass and fall upon someone else."

Astrid had a good idea where that shadow would fall. *I must protect my sisters. It would be nice to have a mighty warrior by your side when you do so.* The rogue thought made Astrid irritable. She shoved it down and stood up.

"Thank you, Ignetha," she said, hugging the homesteader. "It was so good to see you, but now I must be off."

"Good to see you as well. Give my love to the sisters."

"I will." Astrid left Ignetha's yard and headed further into Visby.

This was getting very complicated. How was she to deal with this dangerous man? He had powerful connections, was not alone, and carried magic with him that limited her powers severely. Astrid came to the town square, bustling with the commerce of the day, and stopped. Should I go back?

Astrid was not a coward, but she did wonder if she was up to the task alone. It might be wiser to return with more firepower.

But that would take time, perhaps time we might not have...

Her musings were interrupted by a firm grip on her upper arm and a sharp jerk backward. Just as she was about to cry out, a powerful hand clapped over Astrid's mouth. Before she knew what was happening, she had been pulled into an empty storefront and shoved to the floor.

Astrid's fingers were moving in an incantation when she recognized her abductor. Huw was on the floor as well, practically on top of her.

"Fool of a woman! Did you want Eirik's thugs to cut you down in the street?" he whispered fiercely into her ear, his beard bristling along her neck.

Astrid had a hard time answering his question, having to take a moment to clamp down on the instant response of her body to his closeness, and his hot breath in her ear. She was alarmed at her immediate arousal and took shelter in anger.

"Unhand me, you big oaf! Is your first response always to manhandle me?" The effect of this was somewhat muted by the fact that his hand was still over her mouth.

Huw's eyes were focused intensely on hers. Astrid found this made it difficult to think.

"Come upstairs with me," he said, speaking softly but intensely. "We can talk there without fear of being overheard. Don't shout or make a fuss...our lives are at stake."

Huw's urgency cut through Astrid's anger. She nodded, and he let her go. Astrid followed as Huw crept softly up the stairs and opened a door to a room that faced away from the town square. Once Astrid had joined him, Huw closed the door behind her and sat down on the bed with a sigh of relief.

Astrid remained standing and regarded him coldly. “I’m going to assume, for the moment, that you had a good reason for grabbing me off the street.”

“How kind of you, good lady,” retorted Huw. Astrid was about to snap back at him when he raised his hand in a signal for her to stop. “Eirik’s men are keeping an eye for new arrivals to the town. Word of your presence may or may not have already reached him. Given that the Ironwood seems to be his target, an Ironwood witch alone on the streets of Visby is not safe.”

“My hero,” said Astrid mockingly, but her thoughts were racing.

Clearly, she was running out of time and options. She had no time to go home for reinforcements, but if she stayed here, she would be hunted down by Eirik’s thugs. Huw did not rise to the bait of her words. Instead, he directed a measuring gaze at her. Astrid flushed at his frank appraisal.

“You can’t do this alone, you know,” he said simply.

“It seems that there is no help available,” she shot

back.

Huw stood, and closed the distance between them. “I am here. We will do this together.”

Astrid felt a fluttering in her core, but she couldn’t help herself. “Not worried about witches’ snares anymore?” she challenged.

“I have made…inquiries; those men I ambushed on the forest road among them. I think it is possible Eirik is targeting your sisters. The *bengand* was crafted to destroy your kind. It has no other purpose. The Witches of the Ironwood are amongst the most powerful and are the only witchfolk in proximity. They are a haven for all women who flee the world of men. You would not rest easy in our bed were I to allow something to happen to them. So, it falls to me to protect you and rest of your misbegotten tribe…and don’t think for a minute that little stunt in the forest will go without consequences,” replied Huw, with an angry snarl that somehow morphed into a throaty chuckle that sent a charge through Astrid’s nether regions.

She bit her lip and looked up at the broad-shouldered warrior. “Maybe I’m not sure you’re up to it,” she said quipped.

“Then perhaps I need to prove it to you again,”

Huw said, molding her body to his.

He leaned down and kissed her, demanding her response. Astrid struggle briefly, but as his hard cock pressed against the front of his trousers and fit neatly into the wedge of her thighs and his hand roamed down her back to cup her buttocks, her last bit of resistance melted. She surrendered to his kiss, to his embrace, and to the strong hands that took her body and claimed it as his own.

Huw peeled away the layers of Astrid's clothing, even as she did the same for him. There was something frantic in the way they scrambled for the touch of naked skin to naked skin, standing close together. Astrid could feel his stiffness pressing against her. She reached down to encircle his shaft then gently worked her hand up and down.

"Mmm," she said teasingly, sinking to her knees once more. Her eyes never left his. "Hail and well met, Huw the Jomsviking," she purred, opened her mouth, and placed her lips around the head of his cock.

Huw shuddered with pleasure as Astrid began to work her mouth up and down his shaft. He brought one hand down to snare her hair at the roots at the back of her head. She gave a small moan of mixed pain and pleasure, which only inflamed him further. The bobbing of Astrid's head increased. Huw allowed it to take him to the brink, almost all the way through the gates of his desire, before pulling back.

Astrid looked up at him, questioningly then gasped as he grabbed her beneath her arms and tossed her onto her back on the bed. Huw grabbed her ankles and dragged her across the mattress until her buttocks were at the very edge, her legs on either side of his hips. His throbbing cock was slick with her saliva, and he poised only for a moment at the entrance to her sheath.

Huw's eyes blazed as he drove into her, letting his shaft sink deep into her wetness and warmth. Astrid's eyes opened wide as once again she climaxed from his mere possession of her. He gave her no time to recover as he gripped her hips to keep her close and hammered her pussy relentlessly. Astrid's hands fell back and clutched at the sheets as his cock plunged back and forth, stroking the walls of her pussy. He rode her at a furious pace, reveling in her body's response. Over and over she came, one orgasm following another as she writhed beneath him.

Astrid began to rock her head back and forth, whimpering. "Sweet Freyja...it's too much, too much, too much," she whispered.

Huw smiled grimly. He had allowed himself to let loose, to uncover all of the lust and desire that had built within him for days upon days, and to unleash it all in this full, ruthless act of domination. He was claiming her with his cock, forcing her to submit to his pleasuring, taking command and driving them both higher and higher into peaks of sensation through the unyielding power of the rod between his legs. This was no lovemaking under the furs by the fire. This was fucking, pure animal fucking, the single-minded declaration of what existed for his pleasure.

Astrid cried out his name as Huw finally reached the very pinnacle of his driving frenzy, bathing the walls of her pussy with his thick, creamy essence. The twitching of his cock gave her small, mini-orgasms, as her core spasmed, drawing every last drop of him into her.

Huw stood as solid as granite, his hands under her legs, keeping them around his hips and staying inside her, even as their breathing slowed. He looked down at Astrid and drank in the sight of her: her hair wild against the mattress, her magnificent breasts heaving, her wet lips parted and she gulped in air. He gently let her legs fall as he leaned forward, pinioning her wrists with his hands, until his face was inches from her own.

"You and your witches got it wrong, you know," Huw said softly, almost tenderly. "The gods didn't send me to you. They chose you for *me*. I claim you, Astrid of the Ironwood. I claim you as *mine*."

Drifting, thoroughly spent, Astrid knew that she should offer some defiance, some objection to this idea. Huw was meant to be the champion of the Ironwood, a weapon to be used in a time of danger. But here and now, in the secret places of her heart, she knew it was not true. She was his woman. He had claimed her in the oldest and most binding of ways. It was not a bond to be broken lightly.

Still, she was damned if she was going to let *him* know that. Huw was far too cocksure, both in the metaphorical and literal senses of the term. Instead, Astrid opened her eyes, and eased herself gently from beneath him.

"I'm absolutely exhausted," she said, "and no good to anyone until I have some rest." Pulling the sheets back, she stretched out on the mattress, inwardly marveling at the sweet soreness in her core. No one but Huw had ever been able to do that to her, but again, she was damned if she was going to give him the satisfaction of knowing it.

Annoyingly, she could tell from his smile that Huw had a pretty good idea of how she was feeling, whether she admitted it or not.

"Aye, some rest would be good," he said amiably, joining her on the bed. "There's nothing to be done until nightfall anyway." Huw pulled her into him, taking her in his arms. "Rest now, my delightful witch." He put his head to the pillow.

Astrid was facing away from him, so he could not see the expression on her face. *'My delightful witch,' is it? We'll see about that, you overconfident oaf.* Her tiredness was beginning to leave her body in the face of new ideas that were coming to her.

Astrid waited patiently until the big man's breathing began to slow, and deepen, eventually settling into a low, rhythmic snore. She allowed herself a small inward giggle as she carefully moved out of the bed. *Slayer of villains awake, sawer of logs asleep. Why is it that the strongest of men make the most ridiculous of noises*?

Quietly, she pulled on her clothing, pulling the curtains aside to check the light. The sun hung low in the sky, and afternoon was slowly turning into evening. *Plenty of time.* She slipped out of the room and down the stairs, pulled a cloak off of a peg, and wrapped it around her. Astrid made sure the hood covered most of her face before she opened the door and went out into the street.

The town square was still busy as people went to and fro, many of them heading home to their evening meals after a long day. It was not difficult for Astrid to mix into the bustle and head toward The Sailor's Rest. She didn't have a great deal of information as to what was happening at this point, but The Rest seemed to be at the center of events.

The sun had dropped below the level of the distant mountains, and she was glad that she had taken the cloak. The air chilled quickly, and twilight and evening would come soon. Already, there was a fire burning in the iron brazier that stood at the entrance to The Sailor's Rest, and she could feel its warmth as she went up the wooden stairs and entered the tavern as quietly and unobtrusively as she could.

Fortunately, she had arrived at the same time The Rest was close to its capacity with hungry and thirsty people seeking their fill. Astrid was very familiar with the tavern and managed to find a spot where she could observe the comings and goings, hopefully without attracting notice.

Astrid discovered the error in her thinking within

minutes as she felt the sharp pressure of a dagger in her back, right at the level of her kidney. She smelled foul breath at her ear as a voice behind her snarled, "No trouble, witch. I can see the aura of foul sorcery upon you. I so much as feel a spell, my steel goes in you."

Astrid stiffened, but did not otherwise move as she muttered, "I'll give you no trouble." *Until your knife is away from my vitals*, she added silently. *Then you'll wish you had never been born, you bastard.*

"We're going out the back door," came the growl of her assailant. "No trouble, or it's your blood on the floor." His other hand pulled her from her chair and steered her past the kitchen and out toward the privy. The sudden transition from the heat of the tavern to the chill outside was immediate; the dark had come quickly.

Not good, thought Astrid, *I need to get control quickly*.

She pretended to stumble on the back stairs, and, as she had hoped, her assailant contemptuously shoved her the rest of the way, sending her rolling to the ground. Now that she was away from the immediate danger of his dagger, she used the momentum of her roll to move to a crouch, already muttering the words she needed. Green witchfire darted from her fingers to snake around his neck, tightening like a noose. The ruffian gave a choked-off cry, dropped his dagger, and tried ineffectually to pull at his neck until he fell, unconscious.

Meddle with the Ironwood, get burned.

At a noise behind her, she tried to shift from her crouch to face the new threat. Her quick movement saved her from a brutal blow, but, even so, something heavy caught her on the temple, and sparks filled her field of vision.

I must get away, she thought, even as she fought through the panic and haze. Astrid tried, but simply couldn't bring her mind into the focus she needed to cast a spell. Instead, she spun on her heels, almost fell, but collected herself enough to run down the dark streets of the Visby docks.

She could hear the sounds of pursuit, possibly by more than one person, but she did not dare turn to look. Their movements were skilled and stealthy, which was terrifying. It meant that her pursuers had no wish to be noticed by anyone else, and that meant lethal intentions.

Astrid's head was spinning, and she fought the urge to vomit. She desperately needed to change the dynamics of her situation, to give herself the time she needed to summon her powers and defend herself.

There was a whistling noise, and something passed close to her right ear. She managed to glance over her shoulder as the small axe embedded itself into a post nearby.

Time's up, need to turn this around. Astrid pivoted and bolted directly toward the docks. It was dark, and the jetty was slippery, but she managed to keep her footing as she moved from the packed earth of the town streets to the wooden slats that extended outward into the water.

There was a warning cry from behind her, which Astrid ignored as she came to the end of the jetty, not even breaking stride as she launched herself into the freezing black water.

The cold was a shock to her system, and finally gave her mind and body the wakeup call and clarity she so desperately needed. Astrid could hear the thumping of several feet along the wooden jetty, but she was already underneath it and out of their vision. It would not be long before they put searchers in the water and checked underneath the jetty, but that was all right. She had bought herself the time she needed.

Astrid gripped a wooden piling, concentrated on

slowing her breathing, and closed her eyes.

She muttered the words she needed to meld with the darkness. Once she opened her eyes once again, Astrid knew that as long as she stayed in shadow and was quiet, she was safe from human eyes. The angry voices of her pursuers receded into the distance as she quietly made her way along the docks until she could find a safe spot to pull herself out.

Her teeth were chattering, her blood cold in her veins. It was time to find shelter, and warmth. Astrid scanned the streets, but there was little activity, and no open doors.

Astrid willed herself not to panic. Even though she had thrown her pursuers off the scent, she was in a great deal of trouble. The water had been killingly cold, and, until she could get dry, that same cold still had her in its grasp and would not let go. Already, her body was trembling in a way that told her it would not stop until warmth, or death, claimed her.

A hand gripped her arm, and she spun with as much speed and strength as she could muster, her free hand raised to strike. Before she could do so, it was seized in a strong grip, and she was helpless.

"For Odin's sake, woman!" said Huw quickly and under his breath. "Let's get you warm and dry, or you're done."

Astrid almost sobbed with relief. She had been holding herself together with the last of her strength, and now she simply let go. Huw caught her up easily in his arms and moved quickly through the darkness of the town, back to the house that he had claimed.

***

She's pretty far gone. Huw held her close, feeling her shuddering uncontrollably. Once inside, he stripped her of her clothes and grabbed as many blankets as he could, wrapping her securely in them before setting Astrid down tenderly. Blowing air at the coals and embers in the fireplace, he brought the flame to life as he added new fuel. He wanted as much heat as the hearth could handle.

Alarmed at the lack of response from Astrid, he opened the blankets in which he had wrapped her and noticed her pale skin drained of color.

"Stay with me, Astrid," he commanded.

She moaned in response, but did not open her eyes. Huw pulled off his own clothes and pressed her naked body to his, skin to skin, gasping at the cold emanating from her. He wrapped them together in the bedding and lay down with her in front of the fire. Huw pulled the blankets over their heads as well, just leaving a little bit of space to breathe for both of them. He put his hand on her chest, relieved to feel her heart beating steadily. Next, he checked the beat of her pulse at her neck. It felt weak, but thankfully also steady.

Huw stroked her hair and her face. Holy Odin, what a beautiful woman, he thought as he caressed her. *I knew she was gorgeous, but I don't think I fully appreciated her beauty until now.*

Although she did not open her eyes, Astrid sighed and nestled more deeply into Huw's embrace. She seemed a bit warmer. He hoped so.

Odin, he prayed, willing his thoughts to Asgard, *you know that I and my folk follow your battle-madness. We are your servants. Help me now. Tyr, you know the sacrifices made by the courageous. This woman is brave. Honor her bravery.*

He paused, then added, *Freyja, I know I am not one of yours, but this woman is. Please look after your own.*

Huw closed his eyes, and wordlessly continued to pray.

Time passed. Huw could not tell how long, but when he felt the sensation of fresh air on his face, he opened his eyes.

The fire, the house, even the town was gone. Huw

was on a mountainside on a warm summer day, the temperature pleasantly moderated by a cool breeze. He sat on a slope just at the tree line, a few scattered pines dotting the grass around him, while below him rolled a great forest, dipping down to flank the silvery line of a river in the valley below him.

"Where on earth—" he began, before being interrupted by a familiar voice behind him.

"Perhaps not on earth at all," said Astrid lightly, laughter in her voice.

Huw turned, and there she was, warm and alive and more beautiful than ever. His feelings must have shown on his face because she giggled and tapped him on the nose.

"Well met again, Huw of Hestur. It seems that I owe you my thanks for saving my life."

"You're alive," breathed Huw. "I was worried. I was afraid that the death-cold had claimed you."

Astrid smiled. "You brought me back. When I needed you, you were there, Huw. I will not forget." Suddenly, she laughed. "But that doesn't mean I will make it easy for you. Such is not my nature. I fancy I'll have angry words for you when we wake."

"When we wake?" asked Huw, confused. "So, this is some kind of dream realm. And what do you mean, you won't make it easy for me?"

Astrid laughed again, a delightful sound like a running stream. "In our dreams, you and I may speak freely. This is a place for the heart's truth. But when we wake, we return to our vulnerabilities, our fears, our weaknesses. As I think you may have noticed, I'm rather proud and angry in waking life. You still have to win me. But rest assured, my beloved Huw, I want to be won."

Astrid moved behind him, laid her head against his back, and encircled his waist with her arms.

"You are *my* warrior, Huw, just as I am *your* witch." She hugged him tightly. "This dreaming place is shaped by our love. But now it is time to return to the world. There are villains to be fought"—she poked him lightly in the ribs—"and fair maidens to be won."

Huw sat on the slope, looking out over the vista of mountains, forest, and the valley below, enjoying the cool of the breeze and the warmth of Astrid against his back.

"I don't want to leave here," he admitted, wistfully.

Astrid squeezed his shoulder. "This is the place we earn through our deeds. If we stay brave and true, we will see it again. Now, rest, my warrior. We are needed

Witch and Warrior
in Midgard."

Gently, she pulled him back to rest against her. He closed his eyes, listening to the sound of the wind in the grass.

When Huw opened his eyes again, he looked down to see Astrid nuzzling against his chest, her chest rising and falling in the rhythms of a deep sleep. She no longer felt freezing to the touch and had stopped shivering.

Huw silently thanked the gods. Already, the memories of his dream were fading into faint echoes, and all he could remember was the feeling of deep contentment and love he had shared with the woman in his arms and her assertion she knew she was his...and found no anger or sadness in that knowledge.

Astrid's eyelids fluttered, and she awoke suddenly, sitting up and pushing Huw's chest away.

"What in the frozen Hel..." she muttered, running a hand through her hair. "How did I get here? And where are my clothes?" Astrid's dark eyes fixed upon Huw balefully as she slid further away, covering herself. "Did you bring me here? Why am I naked? Why are you? What have you done?"

Huw looked at her and said nothing. Astrid suddenly felt much less sure of herself than she had a moment ago.

"Come here," said Huw, pointing to his lap.

"What?"

"I said, come here, Astrid. If you're going to be so absolutely willful and ungrateful, I know how to fix that," he said firmly.

"So you can spank me again?" she asked, frozen in uncertainty. "Why on earth would I do that?"

"If I have to put you over my lap myself, it will go the worse for you," Huw warned.

Am I in the wrong here? Astrid wondered. *Have I accused him wrongly*? Memories of the night before were starting to flood back. *Oh, no...*

Huw reached forward to take Astrid by the arm and pulled her to him. She didn't resist.

"Um, Huw, it's quite possible that I overreacted..." tried Astrid, as Huw put her naked body across his lap.

He pressed one of his legs against the back of hers, adjusting her hips so her bottom lay directly beneath his hand.

"Surely, we can discuss this..." Her question turned into a wail as Huw brought his hand down hard on her bare bottom. "I understand that you're angry, but—" She got no further as Huw began to spank her steadily. Kicking her feet in pain and frustration did no good. His hand was relentless, moving steadily over the smooth territory of her firm ass, bringing her sensitive skin from a light sting to a burning heat. She could well imagine when he was done it would be a deep shade of red.

"No!" Her wails only increased the severity of his smacks.

"You disobey me, leave our bed and go into the town on your own," said Huw calmly, as Astrid kicked and squirmed to no avail. "Then you almost get yourself killed, just as I warned you would happen."

Angry tears begin to run down her cheeks, as Huw continued his steady discipline.

"Then I have to save you from freezing to death, warming your unconscious body with my own life's heat," he continued, although she had ceased to struggle and was no longer fighting her punishment.

"And after all is said and done, you *accuse me* of wrongdoing!"

His hand came down to emphasize each and every word.

"I'm sorry, Huw," Astrid wailed through her sniffling.

His hand rested on the soft curve of her buttocks, holding the heat that his discipline had brought against her flesh.

"You're sorry?" he asked sternly.

"Yes," came the muffled response, her head down.

"Then, get up and stand in the corner, facing the wall."

Astrid's head shot up. "What?"

"If you really acknowledge that you've been bad and are sorry for it, get up, and go stand in the corner, facing the wall," repeated Huw.

"I'm *not*—" Astrid got no further as Huw recommenced her spanking, maintaining the same level of severity as he concentrated his discipline on her sensitive sit spots, where her thighs met her buttocks.

"No!" mewled Astrid, writhing and squirming again. "Okay, okay!" she burst out. "I'll go to the corner! I've been bad, and I'm sorry!"

Huw paused. "Keep on being stubborn, and I'll fetch my belt," he warned.

"No, Huw. I'll be good," Astrid sniffled.

Huw helped her up, and she walked shakily to the corner, her bottom radiating heat and pain.

"Lean forward and put your hands on the wall," Huw instructed. "Arch your back and lift your buttocks. I want to see my handiwork."

Astrid seethed a little inside at his commands, but those feelings of indignation were overridden by her confusion and betrayal at how her body was reacting to his discipline and his commands. Part of her didn't want to display herself because she struggled against Huw's dominance, but mostly she was reluctant because she was afraid he would see the evidence of her arousal dripping down her thighs.

Unfortunately, Huw was standing right behind her, the proof positive of his arousal nudging at her swollen labia. He ran his hands down from her shoulders, moving them around to cup her breasts and tweak her nipples. Astrid gasped in mixed pain and pleasure and bit her lip in chagrin as she realized the amount of honey pooling in her core was only increasing.

Huw sighed as he reached her hips, curling his hands around and using one to part her folds while the other pinched and rolled her clit. Astrid's knees buckled, and Huw steadied her. He took a firm grip on her hips and positioned himself, his stiff cock nestling at the entrance to her core.

"*Mine,*" Huw growled, and drove his full length into her.

Astrid cried out in startled pleasure, as a powerful

orgasm wracked her body and, once again, Huw had to steady her as her knees threatened to buckle.

Slowly and steadily, but with a driving rhythm, he began to claim her...again.

Astrid shuddered deliciously and bit her lip as she began to lose herself in the world of sensation. Her hands against the wall anchored her in place, as did Huw's iron grip on her thighs. The rest of her body burned with a series of blossoming fires of pleasure and pain. Huw's pelvis slammed into her backside, reigniting the sting of her spanking. His cock filled her sheath, creating delightful sensations all up and down her interior walls as he stroked her pussy.

Astrid was pinned between the wall and Huw's driving rod, helpless to resist. In that moment, she didn't want to; she wanted to stay in this place forever. She was caught between being driven to higher and higher peaks of pleasure, and a feeling of falling, tumbling into an eternal abyss where time had no meaning, and nothing mattered except the raw, physical reality of Huw's cock pounding her pussy.

At roughly the same point Astrid began to fear that she would never come down from the hurricane that had thrown her into the winds of pleasure and pain, Huw's cock swelled and erupted, sending waves of his cum into her battered core. She cried out as he wrung a final climax from her, the walls of her sheath shuddering.

Huw pulled away from her briefly, only to quickly lean forward and catch her by her waist as she began to fall. He swept her up into his arms, his strength surrounding and holding her. He carried her back to the blankets, laid her down and joined her. He took her in his arms and gently stroked her hair.

"We both needed that, I think," he murmured as he held her. "Seizing at life, to drive away the wraiths of the dark."

There was a smile on Astrid's face as she looked up at him. "When did the Jomsviking warrior become a silver-tongued poet?"

Huw's expression sobered and assumed a faraway look. "Anyone who has faced death has a shard of poetry in his soul, by my reckoning." Then he laughed and shook his head, dispelling his seriousness. "But he saves that either for his time as a graybeard sitting close by the fire or to soothe his woman, else he risks gaining the reputation of a gloomy bastard," he said, his eyes dancing with humor.

Astrid exhaled, long and slowly. "You are right though, Huw," she said, "we did need that." She brushed some strands of hair away from her face. “I’m sorry for my outburst earlier,” she said seriously. “You saved my life. I owe you my thanks, not harsh words.”

Huw chuckled. “Your bottom paid the price for your mouth, and that’s the end to it.”

“Really?” asked Astrid, a bit nonplussed by what seemed like a lighthearted attitude.

He smiled. “My dear witch...” Astrid was surprised as her body tingled with warmth at the nickname “...that’s the point. You did wrong, you paid the price. We’re done. Anything more would be overkill.”

Astrid liked the idea that things could be so easily closed and left behind. She nuzzled her head into his broad chest and murmured, “You make it sound so simple.”

Huw tenderly kissed the top of her head. “Sometimes, things can be quite simple, unless we decide to complicate them.”

Astrid kissed his shoulders. “I like simplicity.” She looked around. “Where are my clothes?”

Huw pointed to a wooden rack near the fire. “They needed drying.”

“Ah, thank you.” Astrid got up and began to dress. “I’m hungry. We could use a meal, and there’s still the matter of the task before us.”

Huw rolled out of the blankets and stood upright. Astrid paused in her dressing to admire the warrior. He was a large man, strongly built, and, as he stood there naked, he resembled nothing so much as a sturdy oak tree, or perhaps a great bear standing on its hind legs. His torso, shoulders, and legs bore an abundance of scars, a testament to both his profession and his longevity. His body left no doubt that he was a warrior who had seen and survived many battles.

Astrid finished putting on her clothes, but did not stop staring at Huw as he dressed.

“How does one even become a Jomsviking?” she asked curiously.

“Don’t you know?” asked Huw. He shrugged. “I thought everybody knew. Dead men’s boots.”

“What does that mean?” asked Astrid.

“When one dies, another may join. The company never numbers more than four hundred. So, if you wish to join our number, you go to the Jomsburg and issue your challenge. If they judge you worthy, one of the Jomsvikings will come out to fight you. You win, you’re in. You lose, you’re most likely dead. Or wish you were.”

Astrid raised her eyebrows. “Not an easy path to follow.”

"The best ones usually aren't. Our way mostly weeds out the braggarts and the secret cowards," he replied.

"According to gossip, you fight only for coin," said Astrid.

Huw shook his head. "That's technically true, but misses the mark by a wide margin. The money...the money is there to keep our weapons and armor of the best, and to demand the respect of those who would hire us. But really, it's about testing yourself. A Jomsviking fights more, and harder, than any other warrior in the North. You have to be very good to start with, and the process makes you even better. And the brotherhood..." He sighed. "It is not a small thing to live surrounded by those like you, whom you would trust with your life."

"We have that in common." Astrid nodded. "And somehow, all of you are immune to witchfire," she said casually.

Huw laughed, and touched the side of his nose. "Professional secrets. Anyway," he said, changing the subject, "how does one become an Ironwood witch?"

Astrid noted his quick shift of topics, but chose not to comment upon it. "We choose those we wish to have sire our children and breed them," she said failing to notice the stiffness of his body and grim look on his face. "The boy-children are fostered off to nearby families in need of sons. The daughters we raise as our own, and they grow into their role in due time."

"And how does one choose a sire for her child?"

"Different ways. My friend Kasia found a strong and fair warrior trespassing in the Ironwood. She spell cast him in order to strap him to a breeding altar and took what she needed from him. When she was done, she ensured he would be safe and then allowed him to go free."

"So that's what happened to Brynn." Huw shook his head. "He could never make hide nor hair of why he'd ended up buck naked in a sacred grove. He was determined to get her back."

"Brynn?" asked Astrid, curious.

"A fellow Jomsviking," explained Huw. "My friend. Told me a wild tale of being kidnapped by magic and seduced into coupling with a Witch of the Ironwood. He made a vow to claim the woman as his own. He can't keep that vow just yet, mind you, but you and your friend Kasia will have much to discuss in the years to come."

"Can't keep it ever, you mean," replied Astrid

tartly. “The Ironwood cannot be found when it does not wish to be.”

“That’s not really the reason and, when the time comes, we have found a way around that. The real reason is that Brynn lies in Jomsburg, fighting for his life.”

Astrid tried to sort through this information. “Why is he fighting for his life? And what do you mean, you *found a way* around the Ironwood’s magic?”

Huw cursed. “It doesn’t matter. We are in need of breakfast,” he said. “Do you have any idea where we can get some without having to worry about knives in our backs?”

“I know someone,” answered Astrid.

Chapter Seven

As Astrid had hoped, Ignetha the homesteader was glad to make them breakfast in exchange for some of Huw's silver. The smell of sizzling back bacon was enough to make her salivate but not so alluring that it drove all of Astrid's questions from her mind.

"So, tell me, Huw," she began.

Huw cursed inwardly. He knew where she was going with this, and he didn't anticipate it going well.

"Aye," he said neutrally.

She leveled her gaze at him. "You know what I'm going to ask."

"I do," he sighed. "Brynn had made his vow, after what your friend, Kasia did, to find her, spank her pretty bottom, take her, and make use of her the way the gods intended. He was angrier than a bear woken out of his winter sleep too early. But, of course, he knew, as we all did and what you said earlier—you can't find the Ironwood if it doesn't wish to be found."

Astrid took a bite of fried egg, which tasted delicious. "But you said that you and your friend managed to find a way around that."

He smiled. "Can't you guess? We found the bone wand, the"—Huw waved his hand in the air—"the *bengand*. There was no way that Eirik ever would have found it. It was a quest and a half and, had it not been so important to Brynn, we would never have undertaken it. Jomsvikings take the choosing of a mate seriously, if they do it at all. Brynn knew two things when he woke, that your friend carried his child...and that she was his. Eirik knifed Brynn while he was sleeping, stole the wand, and slunk off into the night like a thief. That's how *he* got it, with the act of a coward and an oathbreaker."

"*You* were the ones who found it?" Astrid nearly choked on her food. "This thing which threatens the very life of my community?"

"We were," said Huw.

Astrid took a deep draught of water and set her cup down.

"You heedless, mindless, *thoughtless* musclebound boar brain," she said levelly. "My sisters and I all live in fear because of you. All of the Witches of the Ironwood are as mist before the sun when facing that thing."

Well, no more nor less of a response than I

expected. Huw tried to stem his rising temper. *But that's about all I have a willingness to take.*

"First," he said evenly, "if you were a man, your words to a Jomsviking would cause blood to be spilled over them. You've tromped on my patience more than enough. You are to stop now. If you persist in this way, I will put you across that bench you're sitting on and spank the daylights out of you. Second, you call *me* heedless? Why was it that we were looking for the bone wand in the first place?"

Astrid regarded him silently.

"That would be because one of *your kind* thought she'd take a man's seed with no thoughts to his feelings in the matter. She used her magic to tie him down and ride him like he was her personal stud, thinking nothing of working her will upon him! Did she really think that would come without its own consequences? Brynn's a Jomsviking, Astrid. He swore an oath to avenge an insult upon his body and claim what is rightfully his. He wasn't the one who started this."

Behind a stoic face, Astrid's thoughts were whirling and warring with each other. It was true, the Witches of the Ironwood held themselves to be cleverer than everyone else. She and Kasia had laughed over the tale of the mighty Jomsviking bound helpless and madder than a wet hen as she'd ridden him and taken what she wanted. They had given no thought as to what it might have cost Brynn. Kasia hadn't really thought further about it, confident in the protective power of their magics, which, among other things, had freed them from worrying about the consequences of their actions.

And yet...

"I take your point, Huw," she began. "I think you could make a case that Kasia didn't give sufficient thought to using Brynn and stirred the wrath of a powerful man. You made your two points to me. Now, let me make two of my own. First, we're not in this mess because of Brynn's plans, whatever they may have been. You talk of mighty warriors, but, when all is said and done, it's not mighty Brynn that has the bone wand right now, is it? No, he was laid low by a man you call a coward and an oathbreaker. It's a warrior's job to see those dangers coming, and Brynn didn't."

Huw's face turned a dangerous-looking red, and, for a moment, Astrid was afraid he would rise from the table, lose his temper, and subject her to another spanking. The disconcerting part was that not only did her bottom clench in dread, but her sex also pulsed with anticipation and arousal. Instead, after a moment, to Astrid's relief and disappointment, Huw nodded.

"He was betrayed by a man who was supposed to be his brother, but your point is taken. Brynn had the bone wand, and then he lost it. Your judgement is harsh but accurate. Go on to your second point."

Astrid continued. "Secondly, ask yourself why it was that the Witches of the Ironwood had to go to such great lengths to protect our community? Why sacrifice time, energy, and blood to wreak such powerful magics? Because we are women in a man's world, Huw—women who do not wish to bow and scrape and suffer under the heels of boastful and cruel idiots who have less than half our wit and courage. Thus, have we lived for time out of mind, and for this our sisters have made countless sacrifices."

Huw leaned back in his chair and let out a *whoosh* of breath. Astrid looked at him and wondered if he would be sharp enough to see the truth of what she was saying. To her pleasure and surprise, Huw nodded.

"I never thought of it that way," Huw admitted.

"Men usually don't," came the swift reply.

Huw gave a short bark of laughter, and lifted his

cup to Astrid in appreciation of the verbal thrust.

"It seems we understand each other better than we did yesterday," he ventured, eyeing her as he speared a piece of bacon.

"We understand each other better than we did half an hour ago," retorted Astrid.

"That we do," said Huw easily. "So, can we agree to put blame aside and figure out how to find Eirik and deal with him?"

Astrid nodded. "If someone needs killing, he's the man."

Huw chuckled appreciatively. "You've fire in you. Even a fool can see that."

Astrid swallowed the obvious response, along with her bread. After the delicate dance of their conversation, she'd no wish to end up over Huw's knee just for taking an easy, cheap shot.

"So where can we find this villain? I'd have expected him to be right in the middle of last night's affair, but he wasn't," said Huw speculatively.

"Who's this you're looking for?" asked Ignetha as she came and refilled their cups. Her approving squeeze of Astrid's shoulder told the witch her friend had heard at least part of her conversation with Huw.

"Eirik of Jomsburg. Big fellow, dark thatch of hair,

great black bushy moustache," answered Huw.

"Ah." Ignetha nodded. "Word on the waters is that Visby's been made too hot for him, so he's upped stakes and left for somewhere a little more private."

"Any idea where?" pressed Astrid.

"Well, he's been often in the company of Jesper the Half-Dane," ventured Ignetha thoughtfully.

"Jesper has a hall and a farmstead farther up the coast. A little less than half a day by ship, closer to a day by land if you have horses."

"Do we have horses?" Astrid asked Huw.

He weighed the silver in his pouch. "We will soon enough."

***

Late morning saw the pair on horseback, with saddlebags of provisions and supplies as well as a reasonably clear set of directions to the hall of Jesper the Half-Dane. The ostler who had sold them the horses estimated that as long as they kept a steady pace, they would reach the borders of Jesper's farm near sundown.

Neither Huw nor Astrid were experts in horseflesh, but they both had experience in riding, and the animals seemed intelligent and biddable once they had determined that their riders were not hapless idiots. The forest was relatively quiet as they rode.

Astrid discovered to her displeasure that riding and being recently spanked were not terribly compatible activities, but she hid her discomfort as much as she could. She really didn't want to give Huw the satisfaction of seeing her squirm in the saddle. Astrid suspected that he might have had an inkling anyway, as he ordered halts more often than she would have expected. If this was consideration on his part, he was careful not to show it as such, and Astrid felt oddly grateful for that.

The quiet of their journey gave Astrid time to be alone with her thoughts. *He's a remarkable man. For all that I called him a muscle-minded oaf, he isn't one. He listened to what I had to say and genuinely thought about it. The flexibility of his mind is something special. Thankfully, his other parts were far more rigid. Sacred Freyja, he knew how to plow a woman's furrow in a way I've never experienced before. His abilities in the waking world are even better than those in the dream world. He's masterful and, even when he takes me in hand and spanks my ass, my body calls to his. Blessed Freyja, I want this man. Let him be my fate.*

On his horse next to her, Huw's thoughts ran along similar lines. *Always, I think of her. Sharing that time with her on the mountain slope in the dreaming world...I've never felt happier, or more at peace, in all my born days. If I have to fight through a thousand foes to win that future for myself, I'll do so gladly. And our coupling...gods! All other women pale in comparison.*

Huw shifted in his saddle slightly, trying to adjust his stiff cock away from an unyielding saddle, before returning to his thoughts. *And such courage! The way she describes being a woman in a man's world, having to fight with her wits and strength to live as she chooses...what a woman!*

He smiled at the thought of it. He looked up to see Astrid watching him and included her in his smile.

"What pleases you so?" she asked.

Huw coughed and shifted slightly in the saddle. "These are good horses," he said abruptly. "We didn't get cheated on the deal."

"Ah," said Astrid, nodding.

Huw could feel a slight blush creep up his face and hoped his beard hid it or at least Astrid didn't notice it. After a while, Huw reined his horse and came to a stop. He pointed at a rise in the distance.

"A stone ridge, with an ash tree split by lightning at the crest. Unless I miss my mark, that matches the directions the ostler gave us. The Half-Dane's farm starts on the other side of that rise, and his hall isn't far away. From this point on, we need to tread more carefully." Huw dismounted and tied his horse to a thick-trunked tree, indicating Astrid should do the same. "Too much risk of noise," he said. "We'll have to leave them tethered here. Though the possibility that Jesper has dogs concerns me as well," he added, frowning.

Astrid smiled. "I have magics for that. Let me cast a spell, and any dogs will think we are old friends."

Huw raised an eyebrow, impressed. "You're a handy one, aren't you?"

Astrid tossed back, "I'm no deadweight, if that's what you mean."

"If that's what I meant, that's what I would have said," replied Huw easily, checking the tether for his horse, and that there was enough forage within reach for the beast.

Astrid said, "I've yet to see what handy skills you're bringing, anyway."

Huw helped her off her horse, allowing his hand to linger on the curve of her ass. "You are well aware of some, but I have others, and you will see them as well."

Astrid blushed and seemed to focus on her own horse's tether.

As dusk deepened, Huw checked over his gear, making sure nothing clanked loudly, and did the same for Astrid, quickly and efficiently. Astrid performed a muttered incantation and made a ritual pass over both herself and the burly warrior, declaring they would not need to concern themselves with guard dogs.

Huw paused for a moment. "Are you armed?"

"My magics are both sword and shield," Astrid responded.

"But if Eirik is there, with the bone wand..." warned Huw as he unbuckled his belt and passed her a long dagger in a leather sheath. "Put that on your belt. I'm not saying you'll need it, but better to be prepared."

"Thank you." Astrid took the sheathed dagger and threaded her belt through it. The thought of being unable to use her magics made her feel nervous. This was the menace of the *bengand*; it took all the defenses she and her sisters had woven and made them as nothing. *The cursed thing should never have been made. My sisters and I will not be safe until it has been ground into dust.*

"Ready? Off we go, then," said Huw.

He began to quietly make his way up the rise. Astrid followed, not far behind. Moving quietly in a darkened forest was not the easiest of tasks, but Huw managed with seeming ease. Astrid had to concentrate more closely on where she put her feet. As they reached the top of the ridge, next to the shattered ash tree, Huw lowered himself until he was barely above the ridgeline. Astrid, crouched next to him, followed his gaze.

They were at the edge of a series of fields, mostly barley by the look and scent. Less than a thousand yards away stood a group of buildings: a barn, some hayricks on wooden platforms, and a hall, roofed with turf and with torches planted at the entrance.

"Barely a sliver of moon tonight, thank the gods," muttered Huw. "I'd hate to have to cross those fields in full moonlight."

"So, what is your plan?" whispered Astrid. Sound carried in the night, and the noise from the hall seemed to indicate the presence of many people.

Huw's teeth gleamed in the darkness as he grinned. "We're just going to take a look," he replied, and broke into a low, shambling run, crouching low as he made his way across the fields. Astrid cursed as she followed, and soon discovered that there was a knack to running with your back almost parallel to the ground, a knack she did not possess. She gradually fell behind.

Jesper the Half-Dane had set a watchman; a steady enough fellow who shifted his feet back and forth to keep warm, cursing and muttering about missing what sounded like a mighty feast inside. The watchman turned toward the field. It would seem they had not been as silent as they might have liked. He cocked his head as if trying to tell if the sound he heard was simply a rustling of the barley, beast, or man. He leaned forward, and Astrid saw the man collapse as Huw lowered him gently to the ground.

Up close, the sound from the hall carried loudly and clearly. Huw shook his head doubtfully.

"That's a lot of folk," he muttered. "I didn't come here to slaughter someone's whole kith and kin needlessly. We need to be certain that the *bengand* is in there." He looked at Astrid. "Can you sense it? Do you have any way of knowing if it's there?"

"Well, I can try a spell," Astrid whispered.

Huw nodded.

Astrid began an invocation softly, under her

breath, but felt none of the energy flow through her body as she would ordinarily expect. It was like trying to speak underwater. Suddenly, she heard a roar of anger and the sound of smashed crockery, from within the hall.

"Sorcery!" came a furious shout. "Someone tries witchcraft nearby!"

Answering cries of anger added to the tumult within.

"That's torn it," said Huw, drawing his sword. "Run for the horses, Astrid, as fast as you can. Bring them back here. If I should fall, then ride for your life."

"What are you going to do?" cried Astrid.

Huw was already moving, but he stopped briefly to smile at her.

"I'm going to use my handy skills," he answered, just as the door to the hall slammed open and men spilled out. "Now *run*, woman!"

Astrid ran as fast as she could, heedless of the trips and scrapes she suffered as she made her way through the darkness. She hoped she was going in the right direction, but could not be certain.

Behind her, she could clearly hear the sound of clashing blades, and at least one scream. Part of her wanted to go back to Huw, to offer whatever help she could. She could not imagine how he could manage against the multitude that must be spilling out of the hall but reminded herself he was Jomsviking and a mighty warrior.

Astrid gave a cry of relief when the shattered ash tree loomed up in her sight. She stumbled again, descending the slope as swiftly as she dared. The nickering of horses greeted her as she hurried to untether their mounts. Seated on one and holding the reins of the other, she galloped back toward the fray, urging them up and over the ridge.

Her heart was beating quickly. She imagined Huw to be in terrible danger, beset on all sides by murderous foes. As the horses raced across the fields, she could see that at least one of the hayricks was on fire, the entrance of the hall was burning, and, as she strove to determine what was happening, a strange sound came to her ears...Huw was singing.

At first, Astrid feared it was because Huw saw his death and was singing his defiance of his fate. As she got closer, however, she realized Huw was singing from the joy of battle. By the flickering light of the burning buildings, she could see his face, filled with a kind of terrifying elation as his blade cut in deadly arcs and slashes. He was in constant motion as he toyed with his foes, and just when you thought you had figured out where he was going to be next, he would stamp, feint, and reverse. The ring of his slain around him bore silent testimony to the havoc he had wrought upon the hall of Jesper the Half-Dane.

The sound of approaching hoofbeats broke the spirit of the last remaining fighting men, who turned and fled from both Huw and whatever danger this new arrival promised. Huw laughed to see them run then turned and launched himself into the saddle.

His eyes shone brightly as he regarded Astrid and said, “Well done. Now follow!”

Digging his heels into his mount’s side, he spun away from the destruction he had wrought and galloped away. The horses, their nostrils filled with the reek of blood and smoke, were all too eager to put distance between themselves and the perceived danger.

Later, Astrid would look back on that night ride with a smile: the wind whistled in her hair as she flew through the darkness, the crackling sounds of burning behind her, a conquering warrior leading the way in front of her. This was truly the stuff of sagas, and here she was, right in the middle of it. Astrid had never imagined that she would ever be part of such a thing, and it was intoxicating.

When Huw finally signaled for them to halt and leapt to dismount, it was obvious that he, too, felt that sense of intoxication. He pulled Astrid from the saddle and into his arms, drawing her into a deep kiss that pulled them out of their time and place, into their own private world.

Wordlessly, they fell to the ground. Huw flipped up Astrid's skirt then pulled down her stockings using a combination of his hands and his teeth. Astrid unbuckled Huw's trousers, pushing them past his muscular buttocks and down his legs.

He covered Astrid's body with his own, pinning her to the grass as he ran his lips and his teeth across her lips, along her jawline, then down along her throat to the base of her curving neck. His breath was hot on her chest as he thrust into her without warning, taking her in an act of dominance as clear and masterful as his battle-joy had been earlier.

Huw's eyes flashed as he gazed down at her. He had become the subject of all her lustful fantasies and was satisfying them all. His feral smile as he drove into her was at once that of a conqueror taking his prize and that of a lover long been denied his heart's desire. The swift rush of pleasure that accompanied his mounting and breaching her forced small moans and sighs of acceptance and surrender and seemed to drive him further into a frenzy. He grunted and groaned as he pounded her pussy relentlessly, wringing repeated climaxes from her.

"You're *mine*, woman," he whispered fiercely into her ear, accentuating each word with a thrust.

"You belong to *me*."

Without word or warning, Huw switched positions as he lifted her legs so that they rested on his shoulders, her knees nearly at her chest, giving him an angle at which she was completely at the mercy of his ruthless thrusting. And from Huw, there was no mercy to be had. He plowed her savagely, drawing from the same source at the core of his being that fueled his battle-madness.

Astrid felt as if she was in a runaway boat that was racing toward the edge of a waterfall, and that there was nothing that could stop its inexorable fate. Her body arched as if tracing the arc of a great, glittering leap into the sky, before spinning downward into a final, glorious fall from which there would be no return. Huw covered Astrid's mouth before she shattered the night with her cries of ecstasy. Finally, he withdrew his hand and kissed her once again.

"My woman," he sighed. "I thank the gods for you."

"And goddesses," Astrid murmured, much of her still far away.

"And goddesses," agreed Huw, smiling. "Now, we must be up and take shelter in the forest until morning. I've no wish to be found fucking *my* woman in a far-flung field."

"Doesn't sound like the *worst* thing," Astrid muttered, but did not resist when Huw pulled her to her feet.

***

The dawn came some hours later, visiting them both with a welcome warmth. They had not dared signal their location with a campfire, but much of the cold had been kept away by snuggling closely together under Huw's cloak. The horses had not seemed to mind much one way or the other, but Astrid was glad of the sunrise to signal the end of the night's chill.

"So, did you want to see it?" offered Huw.

"I saw it last night," said Astrid wryly.

Huw laughed. "Not *that*, my witch, although it's certainly nothing to be ashamed of. Did you want to see the *bengand*?"

Astrid gasped. "You mean..."

"Seized it last night, right out of some nasty fellow's hands." Huw unlaced one of his horse's saddlebags.

"Was it Eirik?" asked Astrid, recalling the intimidating figure at the center of the elder Witches' predictions.

Huw frowned. "No. Wizened little dwarf of a man, waving this thing around." He handed an object to Astrid.

Astrid gazed at what she held. Originally, it had been a walrus tusk, and it still possessed the heft and smoothness of ivory. It stretched from her palm to the crook of her elbow, curving in a slight arc. The bone wand had been intricately carved, obscure runes blending into smooth lines of beasts and human figures. About a third of the way from the tip, heavy pieces of polished amber had been set right into the wand.

"It's...rather beautiful," admitted Astrid.

"Aye." Huw nodded. He paused and looked more closely then paled. "Great Odin's beard!" he cursed.

"What is it?" asked Astrid in alarm, focusing her eyes on him.

"This is *not* the same bone wand that Brynn and I found, and Eirik stole," he grated, taking it from Astrid and turning it over in his hands. "Loki's balls!" he cursed again. "There must be more than one!"

Astrid felt a sinking feeling in the pit of her stomach. "Does this mean we have the wrong wand?"

"I've no idea. Let's find out. Hand the thing over to me, and try a spell."

Astrid was too rattled to be annoyed at the curt manner of Huw's address to her. Rather, she placed the heavy thing into Huw's hands, and muttered a simple spell for purifying water. Once again, it felt as though she was underwater and could not make herself heard. Both Astrid and Huw gazed on in wonder as the inset pieces of amber on the wand began to softly glow.

"Huh," said Huw, in mingled surprise and distaste. "The wand felt briefly like a living thing in my hand. It was"—he shuddered—"not pleasant."

"There is no way that I can work any magic with that thing near," said Astrid with loathing. "It needs to be destroyed."

"Hmm," said Huw.

Astrid's eyes narrowed. "What does that mean?"

"It means that everything just got more complicated, and uncomfortably so. There are two *bengands*. Who is to say that there are not more?

Where on earth is Eirik, and the other wand? *How* do we destroy these things? What will be unleashed if we try? It seems to me we have more questions than answers."

Astrid's shoulders slumped. "You are not wrong, Huw. This needs more knowledge than we have between us. But where should we seek?"

Huw carefully stowed the bone wand in his saddlebag. "Well, I don't like going backward, but it looks as if we will have to."

"And what does *that* mean?" asked Astrid, a shade exasperated.

"Going back to where Brynn and I stole the first one," sighed Huw, "and finding out more about exactly what we took."

Chapter Eight

Astrid wrapped her sea-cloak around her more tightly and looked over the sea.. According to tradition, the waves were the daughters of the goddess Ran; each daughter was a different kind of wave. As part of her training, Astrid had been made to learn the names of all of Ran's daughters. She leaned over the gunwale and whispered a soft greeting to Hefring, the *lifting-wave* that carried them closer and closer to their destination.

The wind off the sea was cold, but bracing. Astrid delighted in it. She and her sisters were forest-bound for most of their lives, and the chance to ride the whale-road made for a welcome change. The coast of the mainland was still visible to the west as her home isle of Gotland retreated to the south. She wasn't sure how she would feel if all she could see was the sea itself, , yet she knew the great seafarers and the most daring Vikings risked such peril on their long voyages.

Her own voyage was complicated enough. Huw had explained it to her as they had stealthily returned to the burned hall of the Half-Dane, to fetch silver and gold from those whom Huw had slain.

"We will need coin if we wish to make a voyage," he had said pragmatically, as he searched the bodies for valuables. With a certain amount of distaste, Astrid had joined him, recognizing that their need to find answers outweighed her own scruples.

"I did not envision this as a part of my journey," she had observed, grimacing as she pulled a pouch from a corpse's belt.

Huw had shrugged. "I slew them all, so these things technically count as my prize. You're no corpse-robber, if that helps your stomach. Besides, it's a long way to Uppsala, and it won't be cheap."

Astrid had stood upright. "Uppsala?"

The city and its great temples lay far to the north and were not places the Witches of Ironwood were in the habit of visiting. The temple complex was the very heart of the male-dominated priesthood that oversaw and coordinated the worship of the gods throughout the lands. The Uppsala priests and the Witches of the Ironwood were not mortal enemies, but no one would call them friends, either.

"Aye," Huw had responded absently, before he seemed to notice the change in Astrid's tone of voice. He had straightened and looked at her directly.

"They're not my favorite people," he had said apologetically, "and they're unlikely to sing my praises, after my last encounter. But they are the ones most likely to possess the knowledge we need."

Now Huw joined her at the gunwale, looking over the ocean to the coastline they were approaching. "Half a day, and we'll dock at Sigtuna," he said. "Two days' journey into the interior, and we'll be at Uppsala. A day, if we can get horses."

Astrid nestled into his reassuring bulk. "Do we have a plan?" she asked, half joking. The Jomsviking made most of his decisions on the spur of the moment, as far as she could tell.

Huw seemed to have taken the question at face value. "You might be the one taking the lead here," he said frankly. "If the priests recognize me, not only will they not say a word, they're more than likely to set their guardians on me. I've handled them before, but it doesn't get us any closer to the knowledge we seek."

"Any ideas on how I pry the information from them?" asked Astrid, skeptically. "They're not exactly the kind of folk to spill their secrets in a bar or a bed nor are they great admirers of the Witches of the Ironwood."

Huw made a noise between a chuckle and a growl.

"They may not be great admirers of your sisterhood, but from what I've heard, you'd be wrong on the other two counts." He put a possessive arm around her shoulders, drawing her into him more tightly and added, "But I'll see Uppsala burn before I let one of those soft-fingered priests lay a hand on you."

Astrid blushed, not entirely displeased by the gesture or his words. "I didn't know you felt that way," she murmured.

"Since I first saw you," he said, low and fierce. He gave her shoulder another squeeze. "Haven't you heard me? You're mine."

Astrid did not argue with him. She wasn't sure that she wanted to. *There are worse things in the world than being claimed by a handsome warrior. It wasn't the destiny I had planned for myself, but wise women know that the gods laugh at mortal plans. Still, I can't imagine giving up my life in the Ironwood. It's all I've ever known! And I don't see this fellow living meekly under the rule of my elder Sisters. But leave him? Never see him again? I'm not sure that I can do that, either.*

"So," continued Huw, "we have to consider how you worm secrets out of a temple priest without sharing a bed with him."

"Well," said Astrid speculatively, "there's always the promise of a bed, without follow-through."

"No," said Huw flatly, shaking his head.

"Huw, trust me, witches are very good at this sort of thing!" Astrid pressed. "We know how to find the weaknesses in men."

"Good for you. The answer is still no."

"Do you have a better idea?" demanded Astrid.

"Yes. Burn Uppsala to the ground before spanking you for your willfulness."

"It's like talking to a child," said Astrid in disgust, trying to pull away.

Huw, however, kept her held close to him. "Not so," he murmured in her ear, his hot breath causing her core to tingle. "For a child could not bend you over the gunwale, spank you soundly, and take you in front of the entire crew."

Huw's hot whisper sent arousal surging throughout her body. The warming rush had become something with which she was all too familiar. Turning her body into his, she plucked at his cloak and said softly, "I would be a fool to say that you would not dare, for I know you most certainly would."

"You're right in that," agreed Huw, gazing down at her fiercely.

"Then all I can hope for is that my Viking lord waits until we have a room in Sigtuna, and that he will discipline me for pleasure, not punishment." Astrid looked up, wide-eyed.

A rumbling chuckle began, deep in Huw's frame. "Your words please me, my witch." He turned her to face the water, allowing him to press the weight and stiffness of his hidden cock against her ass. "Let the daughters of Ran make quick work of the rest of our journey."

***

For all of its size, Sigtuna had a different atmosphere than Visby. While Visby was a busy port city, it was still a community, with homesteads and outlying farms, and a central square dominated by the business of locals.

Sigtuna, however, was all about comings and goings, and the locals made their livings by seeing to the needs of those who came and went, not those who stayed. By far the most traffic was created by pilgrims on their way to and from the temple complex at Uppsala.

Huw and Astrid disembarked and tried to mingle with the steady stream of people leaving the docks, toward the inns and marketplaces.

"By the gods, everybody seems to be on the move to somewhere else!" Huw snorted, keeping a tight hold on his possessions in the crowded streets.

"Not everyone," murmured Astrid, her eyes scanning the mass of people carefully. "Examine the scene like you would a battle, Huw."

"Hmm." He followed her advice, and started to get a sense of the ebbs and flows of movement around the docks. As he did so, Huw also noticed those who dipped into and out of the crowd, like kingfishers after their food—cutpurses and pickpockets, no doubt. There were also the touts, who appraised the newcomers with hard eyes, selecting likely arrivals to lure to the dice rooms and other pleasures.

"A lot more watchers than I would have thought," Huw admitted. "Best get ourselves off the streets and into a room, before we attract too much attention."

"That's one good reason," said Astrid with a grin. "I can think of another."

There were many establishments that catered to the temple traffic, and, since it was not the time of a great festival, there were rooms to be had. Huw selected one on the second floor, with a window overlooking the inn's stable yard.

"Odin's beard!" he said, relieved to be away from

the press of people. "Can you imagine what the crowds must be like during the summer solstice, or Yul?" He unbelted his tunic and tossed his gear and weapons onto a chair.

"Fortunately, it's just the two of us here," observed Astrid innocently.

Her tone caught Huw's attention, and he smiled. "Aye. You make a good point, witch," he said, lifting off his tunic. Bare chested, he strode over to the bed where Astrid sat.

The heat from her gaze told him she enjoyed his muscled bulk, and she used his thick forearm to pull herself to her feet. She lightly kissed the middle of his chest, nuzzling the curly down on his skin.

"I could never stand a hairless chest," she murmured into him. "I want a man as my bedmate, not a boy."

Her shiver at the rumbling chuckle that came from deep within him gave him happiness. "No fear there, my witch," Huw laughed. "My boyhood's long behind me."

"So I see," said Astrid, looking up at him.

Placing her fingernail where her lips had been, she drew her finger down from the middle of his chest, along the line of his hair, to the waistline of his trousers. She bit her lower lip and slipped her fingers into the waistband. Huw said nothing, but gazed down at her, filled with lust.

Without breaking her gaze, Astrid pulled his trousers down to his ankles, sinking to her knees to do so. The evidence of his lust sprang free, standing proud and erect. Still looking into his eyes, Astrid slid her hands up the columns of his muscled thighs, around his buttocks, and wrapped the fingers of both hands around his shaft. Huw took a deep breath, stifling a moan.

"My Odin," said Astrid huskily, "your Freyja is here, to offer worship."

Keeping the fingers of one hand circled firmly around the base of his cock, her other hand gently cupping his balls, Astrid slowly took Huw's entire length into her mouth, sliding her lips along his shaft until she was at his groin. He was delighted to see her shudder as she pulled back, equally slowly, until she released the head of his cock with a slight pop, looked up at him, and lasciviously licked her lips.

"Does my prayer please you, mighty one?" asked Astrid demurely, from her kneeling position.

Huw felt as though he was burning up "Don't you dare stop," he growled.

"Of course, my lord," purred Astrid, and began the work of sucking his cock in earnest. At times she would pump, running her mouth quickly up and down his length, while at others, she would use her encircling fingers up and down, concentrating a flicking and darting tongue at his engorged tip. Astrid ran her tongue slowly along the underside of shaft and lapped gently at his balls. She seemed to be enjoying her sense of control. That was an illusion...one he would shortly dispel for her.

Huw closed his eyes and let her service him. His body stiffened in anticipation of his release. Exerting his control, his powerful hands came down to tangle into her hair, and Astrid gasped as Huw held her head in an iron grip and began thrusting into her mouth. His cock hit the back of her throat and Astrid relaxed it completely, submitting to his fucking her mouth with wild abandon.

His hands tightened even further as his whole body shuddered, shooting ropes of creamy cum past her tongue and down her throat. Astrid worked her lips and tongue to draw every last drop from him. Huw, who had squeezed his eyes shut at the moment of his release, opened them to look down at Astrid, who smiled up at him as she circled her lips with her tongue, making sure she had swallowed everything.

"Such a naughty witch," he chuckled appreciatively. He put out his hand to help her rise to her feet.

Astrid teased, "If I'm such a naughty witch, then I wonder what comes next."

"You have far too many clothes on. Remove them...now," he growled.

He sat at the edge of the bed, fully naked and already beginning to stiffen once again. Astrid was smiling as she stripped. *Gods, my woman is magnificent.* Her skin was pleasingly smooth, and her waist was trim before blossoming into magnificent curves of breasts and buttocks. Just the sight of her removing her stockings was enough to make him want to spread her legs and give her a rough plowing. But that could come later. She had asked for a pleasure spanking, and she would get one.

Huw guided the stunning woman across his lap and felt his cock spring back to full hardness as she settled in. Astrid giggled. "I guess you're happy to have me here, my lord."

"You might well say so." Huw allowed his hand to sail over the billowing curves of her ass.

With his other, he reached down and tugged at her

nipple, causing Astrid to moan and squirm a little. Huw took that as his opportunity to begin to lightly pepper her bottom with smacks.

Astrid sighed happily and wiggled her ass. “So much better than punishment.”

“Behave properly, and you won’t be punished,” said Huw gruffly.

“Yes, my lord,” replied Astrid, raising her bottom slightly and spreading her legs a little wider in blatant invitation.

Seeing her skin begin to pinken, Huw slightly increased the tempo and force of his spanks, listening to her happy sounds before he slipped his hand between her legs and found her clit. Astrid gasped and lifted her hips still higher. As he tugged and rolled her swollen nub, she pressed her pelvis against him. Huw withdrew and began once more to smack her bottom.

“Naughty,” he remonstrated. “Good things come to those who wait.” He ran his hand along her ass, kneading her flesh.

“But I don’t want to wait,” Astrid pouted. “Why should I have to wait?”

Huw once again increased the speed and intensity of her spanking. Astrid squirmed a little more, in response.

"Because it pleases me, and that's the only answer you need," he responded firmly, lightly spanking her sensitive sit spots.

"Yes, my lord," responded Astrid meekly. "As you wish."

"That's my good witch," said Huw, using his fingers to spread her labia before penetrating her wet sheath with two fingers.

"Mmmm," said Astrid, shuddering happily.

"See? What did I tell you?" Huw crooked his fingers slightly to find her pleasure spot.

"Yes, my lord!" answered Astrid, with a gasp.

As he stroked her, he watched and felt the rush of her climax come like a sudden wave. She moaned, pressing herself against him, squeezing her thighs together.

Huw withdrew his fingers, covered in her honey, and slid her own wetness across her clit, circling her pleasure center. Astrid shivered as she came a second time. She was still in her own world as Huw lifted her up and set her on her back on the bed.

"What are you..." Astrid began before she slammed her head back on the pillow, moaning.

He put his head between her thighs and let his tongue run languorously between her nether lips before darting at her clit. Astrid's legs were pressed closely against Huw's head, and he exerted his strength to once again part her thighs and have her pussy at the mercy of his mouth and tongue.

"Huw!" she cried, as another orgasm rushed through her body.

He sensed her discomfort at the loss of control, but he would teach her to accept any and all pleasure he chose to give her. He chuckled with his mouth pressed against her, and the sheer vibrations of it brought her to the apex point, and over, yet again. His Astrid was a woman of tremendous capacity and response. He drew back and flipped her onto her belly, pulling her hips upward to lift her pussy into position. He smiled as he regarded the incredibly erotic vision of his woman, face down and bottom up, presented for his pleasure.

"Hold on, my witch," he growled, as he drove his cock to the very end of her soaking sheath. Astrid cried out as he sank his shaft into her depths, slamming balls deep into her.

The time for erotic play was over, thought Huw, his lips curling into a snarl. It was time for pure animal fucking, the freeing of the civilized aspects of his nature. These were some of the last coherent thoughts that he had, as he lost himself in the raw act of claiming his woman.

He fucked into her over and over, denying her the ability to think. She had surrendered to the simplest, most basic thing: her warrior had taken control of her body, claimed her, and was using her for his pleasure. In the process, Huw was certain he had driven her past anything she had ever experienced. Astrid was screaming into her pillow, crying his name, begging him not to stop while telling him she couldn't take anymore. She had long since passed any sense of anything she was saying.

He plunged his cock into her, dragging it back out, reveling in the feel of her cunt closing around it, fighting for her pleasure and to keep him within. She was built for pleasure. The flare of her hips meant he had a good strong handle to hold her in place while he rode her hard. She had tried to rise on all fours, but Huw pushed her back down as he slapped her ass...this time with a bit more sting.

Finally, after they had climbed further than they could have ever thought possible, Huw exploded in a final, convulsive burst, bathing Astrid's battered pussy in an eruption of his creamy essence, holding onto the pinnacle of his ecstatic release, before sinking to the bed. Astrid let her knees slide down, unable to move any farther before closing her eyes and falling immediately into an exhausted slumber.

Throughout the night, each time he reached for her, she responded with wild abandon. Huw didn't remember a time he had lusted for a woman the way he did Astrid. Each time he woke hard and in need of her softness, he told himself he should take a care not to use her to the point she had trouble walking. But it was like he was a lad once again in the first flush of sexual awakening and he couldn't seem to satisfy his need for her.

***

Birdsong at dawn finally broke through Astrid's deep, dreamless sleep, and she opened her eyes to see Huw's broad shoulders moving up and down in the rhythm of his own sleeping. Astrid rolled up on the edge of the bed and felt the night's excesses in every muscle of her body, but most especially in those that had responded to Huw in a such a visceral way. Over and over during the night he had reached for her, drawing her beneath him before mounting her and stroking her to ecstasy. Ignoring her body's protests, she quietly slipped out of bed and pulled on her blouse and skirt before going to the window to get her first look at the day.

It was not long past dawn, but things were already moving in the bustling port of Sigtuna. A stable boy hurried across the inn's courtyard with a bucket of oats. A girl from the kitchen headed toward the sewer, struggling with a heavy tub of dirty dishwater. Astrid watched the stable boy briefly set his bucket down to help her, smiling. The girl smiled shyly back as the boy took one side of the tub.

We can't help ourselves, can we, thought Astrid, as she watched the scene play out below her. *We seek connection, we seek love, friendship. We crave it.*

The lead stablehand came out and cursed as he saw the bucket of oats sitting in the middle of the courtyard. The boy rushed back to pick it up, ducking a cuff to his head with the ease of long experience.

It doesn't matter if it's unwise, or dangerous. The connection makes it worthwhile. Astrid turned and looked back at the bulky, recumbent form of the warrior she had shared a bed with. She smiled, removed her clothes and returned to bed to curl into his warmth.

***

Both Huw and Astrid were ravenous and consumed their breakfasts quickly and with little conversation. Huw grinned as he mopped up the last of his fried egg with a piece of fresh bread.

"By Sif's golden hair, woman, that was a night beyond imagining," he said in contentment.

"I've never had the like," agreed Astrid, smiling at him.

"I should bloody hope not!" Huw responded emphatically. "Anything past that is the provenance of the gods, I think."

He surveyed the table to see if there was anything he might have missed. Just as he noticed a last, solitary piece of bacon, Astrid snaked out a hand to seize it and popped it in her mouth.

"Unfair!" Huw cried out. "How do you expect me to keep in such mighty form without sustenance?" He slapped his own midriff for emphasis.

Astrid chewed, swallowed, and then stuck her tongue out at him. "With one less piece of bacon than he might have had," she teased.

"Spankings have been given for less," grumbled Huw, shaking his head.

"Careful, mighty warrior. Promise to spank me again like you did last night, and I'll steal the food right out of your hands." Astrid giggled.

"Not all spankings are equal," warned Huw, with

heavy emphasis.

"They couldn't be, or no woman would behave herself across the entire North," Astrid responded tartly.

Huw and Astrid regarded each other for a moment, then burst into laughter.

"Point taken," said Huw, clapping his hands on his thighs before standing up.

"So are we any closer to a plan?" asked Astrid.

"Yes. Find a priest and throttle him until he tells us what we want to know."

"While that approach has much to recommend it," said Astrid, "I was going to suggest taking a look at the temple library."

Her suggestion was met with silence, until Huw finally said, "The what?"

"Uppsala is a center of learning as well as worship," replied Astrid. "There may well be written records of the bone-wands—how they were made, how they work, how they can be unmade."

"And you think all of this will be written down? Where anyone may read it?" Huw frowned.

"Well, it's not that simple. First, there's not all that many who know how to read and write." A thought struck Astrid. "Can you read and write, Huw?"

"I manage," he replied stiffly.

We'll call that a no, but I don't want to injure his pride, so we won't say so out loud.

"I've been more formally trained, so my abilities are well shaped," said Astrid carefully. "At any rate, there's also the fact that religious libraries are not usually open to the public. People like to keep a close hold on their secrets, priests as much as anyone else."

"So you suggest that we gain access to this library, one way or another," said "Does one of these libraries contain a great number of books?"

Astrid nodded.

"So how can you be sure of finding the right book?" asked Huw, with a shade of triumph in his voice, as if he was clinching an argument. "Taking a priest and tickling his toes with hot coals is better."

"But how can you be sure of finding the right priest?" returned Astrid. "And even if you do so, how can you be sure he's telling the truth?"

"They always tell the truth, eventually," said Huw darkly.

"I don't think that will get us what we need, my warrior," said Astrid, smiling at him. "Cunning is the blade that will get us what we want here, I believe."

"Cunning with a sword behind it," murmured

Huw.

Astrid put a hand on his shoulder. "Both work best when they work together."

Huw nodded. "To Uppsala, then."

***

Huw adjusted his perch on his saddle, and checked to make sure Astrid was close behind him. They had purchased horses from the inn, although Huw hadn't been completely happy with the transaction. The lead stablehand had been a sullen bastard, and Huw hadn't liked the look of him. They had paid nearly twice what horses had cost in Visby, which the stablehand attributed to the higher demand, what with all the pilgrim traffic.

Huw had handed over the necessary coin with a grumble and had left the courtyard before a gray-cloaked man came up to consult quietly with the stablehand.

The road was busy, not absolutely packed but filled with enough traffic that Huw and Astrid had to weave between pedestrian pilgrims. Huw kept an eye on the sky, where clouds were forming to the west.

"Let's hope there's no rain," he said over his shoulder to Astrid. "I don't want to think about what this road would become."

"Nothing very pleasant," agreed Astrid. "How far to Uppsala, do you think?"

"Less than half a day."

The time passed with relative ease. The threatening clouds stayed in the west, and the foot traffic thinned out as the pair left Sigtuna further behind them. They rested once by a stream, to give the horses time to forage and drink, and take a break from their time in the saddle.

Astrid rubbed her bottom and walked around, munching on an apple and stretching her legs. "I'll not deny that horseback makes this trip easier and quicker, but I don't think I could ever get used to life in the saddle."

Huw scooped some water from the stream, running it through his hair and beard. "Some of my brothers in Jomsburg served a term with the emperor, down in Miklagard," he said. "They spoke of enemies who lived on horseback. They drink mare's milk and weep like children when their horses die."

Astrid shook her head. "No thank you, not for me. Especially if you're going to keep spanking me."

Huw nodded. "We may have to get you a special pillow," he said, half in jest.

Astrid eyed him. "Or you could spank me less.

Maybe just pleasure spankings. How does that sound?"

"Like a girl who wants to get away with misbehaving."

"You're hopeless," said Astrid, as she put a foot in the stirrup and lifted herself onto her horse.

Huw saw Uppsala in the distance well before they arrived. Its many temples were built higher than any home or mead-hall he had ever seen. He wondered if Astrid had seen anything so grand. One hill in particular was dominated by a circle of tall, wooden god-poles.

Huw stopped briefly, taking in the carven poles, roped together to form an enclosure, that stood starkly against the sky. "The Uppsala Vé," he breathed. "Love or hate the priests, you cannot deny the power of the gods."

"Or the goddesses," murmured Astrid.

Huw smiled at her. "Or the goddesses, indeed. Let us hope that all of them may smile on our enterprise."

"Speaking of Miklagard, I have heard that their emperor tells them to worship only a single god, and they obey him," observed Astrid.

"I wonder which one," mused Huw. "But who can reckon with the ways of foreigners? Let's move on," he shrugged. "It would be good to find a place to stay

Witch and Warrior

before darkness falls."

Chapter Nine

The atmosphere within the Uppsala inn at which the pair managed to find lodging was very different compared to their stay in Sigtuna. While the port city had been filled with a bustling sense of comings and goings, Uppsala seemed more sedate, and people seemed very self-contained.

"As sociable as a graveyard, and maybe less so," grumbled Huw into his ale.

"It must be different during festival times, but this...this will make it harder to make any kind of inquiries," agreed Astrid.

"Well then," said Huw, draining his cup and wiping his beard, "I reckon it's time to visit an old friend. Come."

He got up from their table in the common room and went out into the street, with Astrid following. Unlike most towns or cities they had known, the streets of Uppsala were lit up at night by torches standing at regular intervals.

"Must cost a fortune in firewood," observed Huw, as they made their way from the inn.

"It does look nice," said Astrid. "Certainly speaks to the wealth of the city. I wonder why they do it?"

"Helps drunken priests stagger their way home," said Huw wryly.

"You really don't like them, do you?" asked Astrid, eyeing the shadows as they walked. With her spellcasting abilities dampened by the presence of the *bengand*, she felt more vulnerable than usual.

"Every man–or woman–should make their own peace with the gods and live accordingly. I don't trust people who grow fat on the labor of others. Don't get me wrong, I've known some damn fine men who were priests. I've fought alongside some in battle and trusted my flank to them. But a whole great collection of them doing nothing but living off the donations of others? Too much opportunity for corruption and mischief."

"Some would say the same thing about the Jomsvikings," observed Astrid.

Huw stopped. For a moment, Astrid thought he was going to lose his temper, but she relaxed as she realized that he was only thinking about what she'd said and considering his response.

"They might say that indeed, my witch." said Huw as they set forth down a different street. "But they'd be wrong. Jomsvikings don't live off the charity of the pious or the foolish, but the pay we earn with our sweat and our blood. Any man who doesn't like what we do or how we do it is welcome to lay out the hazel rods and challenge any one of us to combat or do the job himself. Can these priests say the same?"

"Lay out the hazel rods?" asked Astrid, curious.

Huw smiled grimly. "To make a square on the ground, six feet by six feet. A fighting enclosure, for the *holmgang*–formal combat. Two men enter, one man leaves."

"That's quite a way to live, knowing that you could be challenged by anyone, at any time," said Astrid.

"Keeps you sharp," replied Huw. "Ah, here we are."

He had stopped before a house with a wooden frame and a thatched roof. There was little to distinguish it from other houses, aside from the fact that next to the door had been hung a block of wood, with *jera*—the rune for the letter J—carved prominently into it.

"Sign of a home with a retired Jomsviking living there," said Huw, pointing to the block.

"I've never seen that before." Astrid, looked at it curiously.

Huw laughed. "Not many retired Jomsvikings." He walked up to the door and gave it a sharp rap.

"Guthrum! Wake up, you dozy bollocks! It's Huw of Hestur!"

Astrid had to suppress a laugh at Huw's manner of greeting. It seemed to be effective, however; she heard movement within, and a voice heavy with age said from behind the door, "If you're Huw of Hestur, then you'll know the name of the ship we landed at Hedeby while it was half on fire."

Huw laughed, a deep belly laugh Astrid had not heard from him before. It made him sound like a much younger man. "The Wave-Splitter. Gods above and below, I was practically a boy when we made that raid."

The door opened to reveal a man stooped with age and leaning on a cane, his iron-gray hair hanging down in long braids, his leathered face wrinkled with a broad smile. His left eye had a patch of black leather over it. "You're still practically a boy, young Huw," said the fellow, chuckling. "Come in, come in, and put the dark behind you."

Before he entered his friend's house, Huw stepped back and gestured to Astrid, who bowed slightly. "Guthrum, may I introduce my companion, Astrid of the Ironwood."

Guthrum's lone eye gleamed brightly as he regarded the woman. "Of the Ironwood, you say? Well, hail and well met, my dear. My house is graced by your beauty." He gestured inside.

"Better manners than you," murmured Astrid to Huw as she stepped over the threshold. She sped up slightly to avoid the expected smack on her bottom, but he caught her anyway.

Guthrum closed the door and bolted it. "Be welcome in my house," he said with easy courtesy. "My housekeeper has gone home for the night, but I have some bread and cheese. And mead, of course. The young fellow here can see to anything else you may require; my old bones need the fire's warmth after nightfall these days."

Guthrum lowered his frame into a comfortable chair set near the fire. Astrid was certain that he once must have been a massive man. For all his age, Guthrum looked more like a perching great eagle than anything else. His house was cozy and warm, there was an abundance of furs and pillows, and it bore the evidence of a man who had used his wealth carefully and well, to build a place of comfort.

Huw found a seat for Astrid before taking out

three horn cups and pouring generous portions of mead into them. After he had passed them out, all three raised their cups, and Huw said, "To the joy of seeing old friends once again. Skál."

"Skál," they responded, and drank.

Guthrum gave a contented sigh as he leaned back and regarded the pair sitting across from him. For all of his age, and despite his missing eye, Astrid had the feeling that old warrior missed little.

"Would I be right in guessing this is your second recent visit to Uppsala, young man?" he asked shrewdly.

Huw chuckled into his cup, shaking his head. "Clever old bastard. How did you know?"

Guthrum's lone eye gleamed triumphantly. "The priests tried to hush things up, but I still know a few people. And the whole affair bore all the hallmarks of you, or someone like you. Not alone, though, as I recall. Did this lovely young lady accompany you the last time you were here?"

"Nay. It was Brynn."

"Ah." Guthrum nodded. "So, you stole a *bengand*, as I understand it."

Astrid looked at him sharply. Huw raised an eyebrow. "You are very well informed," he said carefully.

"Live in this troubled world for long enough, you learn a few things," observed Guthrum drily.

Astrid decided to take the initiative herself. "And in your time, noble sir, have you learned much about the bone wands?"

Guthrum turned his piercing eye on her. She smiled sweetly in response.

"I don't blame you for wanting to know, for they concern you and your kindred closely. But we'll come to that in a moment. What I am curious about, Huw, is why you and Brynn chose to risk your lives to obtain one."

Huw took a sip of mead. "To come to the heart of the story, Brynn was insulted and used by a Witch of the Ironwood. He sought to avenge the insult and claim the woman properly. I was merely assisting him as a friend should. At the time, I failed to understand his obsession, as one warm, wet sheath is pretty much the same as another...or so I thought. I now know differently."

Gunthrum smiled. "It would appear that the business has widened, if I'm not mistaken."

"You are not," admitted Huw. "Brynn lies fearfully wounded, stabbed as he slept by Eirik Skallagrimsson, who has broken his oath, taken the *bengand*, and intends some broader evil against the Ironwood, the extent of which we do not know. While we are still hunting him down, we came across this."

Huw pulled the second bone wand out of his satchel and handed it to the old warrior. Guthrum ran his hands along the length of the walrus tusk, peering closely at the carvings and pieces of amber.

Astrid shivered involuntarily. The artifact carried a sense of something alien, a kind of indescribable *wrongness*, with it.

Guthrum noticed her reaction, but did not comment. He handed the wand back to Huw, who returned it to his satchel.

"Not the same one as was stolen from you," Guthrum said flatly.

"No," said Huw, shaking his head. "Another. With its capture, we felt that we were swimming in deeper waters than we had known and needed further knowledge. And wisdom, hopefully," he added.

Guthrum sank more deeply into his seat. To Astrid, he seemed to be looking within himself. "I know someone who could add to what you know," he said finally. "Whether or not he has any wisdom to add is yet to be seen. But that is a visit for the morrow; it is too late to see him tonight. Please do me the honor of taking shelter under my roof. There is a room the housekeeper uses, when she has stayed over late and needs to spend the night. You may make use of it tonight. I assume the two of you will be sharing it."

Huw and Astrid glanced at each other, and Guthrum laughed. "Permit an old man his mirth, and take solace in the fact the walls are thick, and I am hard of hearing."

Astrid blushed, but couldn't help also smiling at the retired warrior. In his rough way, he was rather charming.

The hawk-faced veteran returned her smile. "Up you get, the both of you. I'll sit by the fire a while, and wake you in the morning. The elderly need less sleep than the young, for some reason."

Huw drained his cup and stood up, nodding respectfully to his old friend. "In the morning, then. Thank you for your hospitality, Guthrum."

Guthrum waved a hand airily as Astrid stood and thanked him as well. "Make sure to use some of the night for sleep!" he admonished them.

They both laughed quietly as they went up the stairs. The housekeeper's room was simply furnished, with a bed, a chair, and a dresser. But the blankets were thick, and the mattress comfortable, a marked improvement from anything either of them had slept upon recently. It was cold enough that both of them were quite chilly by the time they had undressed, and they happily snuggled into each other.

Astrid shivered a little as she laid her head on Huw's broad chest. "Getting cold reminds me of that horrible night, when I almost died."

Huw stroked her hair. "I am sure, my witch. But you're safe now, and hopefully your own bottom will remind you to avoid such foolishness in the future."

Astrid ran a hand along the muscles of his midsection. "You're awfully confident in the teaching power of your hand," she teased.

"Perhaps. Or perhaps I'm just willing to continue to provide as much instruction as needed."

"Do you like spanking me?" she asked, curious.

Huw kept stroking her hair, and nodded. "I do. I like everything about it. The way you look when you're across my lap, the sound it makes, the feel of your ass, the way you squirm, the way you get aroused and ready to fuck..."

"You do make it sound very appealing," murmured Astrid, sliding her hand farther down his center line, until her questing fingers found his cock. It was already hard. "And clearly, yes, it does appeal to you..."

Huw's breathing became shallow as Astrid let her fingers gently skim along his length, back and forth. "There are other things I find appealing as well," he murmured.

"Like this?" she asked, softly kissing his chest and his stomach as she tightened her grip on his cock, moving her hand up and down.

His only reply was a soft groan. Astrid worked her way down his body, arrived at her destination, and lightly kissed his balls, feeling him stiffen, and then took the head of his cock in her mouth, swirling around it with her tongue.

Huw laughed softly. "You'll awaken the beast," he said.

"That's what my magics are good for," Astrid replied, before returning to her worship of his cock.

She took his length in her mouth, sucking tightly. Huw reached down to tangle his fingers in her hair and pulled her head up again before rolling atop her and settling himself between her legs.

"Be careful what you wish for," he said, low in this throat. "I know a few spells of my own."

He raised himself from the burrow he had made

and began his own journey down the length of her body, pausing at each nipple to lightly suck and bite, before kissing his way down her belly, stopping at her mons. He dipped his head between her legs, making his tongue broad as he drew it up her labia, before darting at her clit, flicking it and taking it gently in his mouth.

"Sacred goddess," murmured Astrid as she clutched the sheets and writhed.

She could move her upper body, but Huw had her lower half firmly pinned as he pushed his tongue past her nether lips and into her warm, wet core. Her honey coated his beard as he gave his full attention to her swollen clit, licking at it before taking it into his mouth and sucking at it while swirling his tongue around."

"Huw," gasped Astrid, half pleading.

He chuckled before nipping her engorged nubbin and straightening up, bringing his throbbing cock in line with her entrance. Astrid gave a little whimper of longing as she felt the head of his cock part her labia, gasping as she felt him lift her legs onto his shoulders, so that she was half suspended in the air, helpless.

Huw entered her with one vigorous thrust, and Astrid cried out as his stiff rod buried itself within her. Uncontrolled, her body responded with a rushing orgasm, so wet she was sure she must have soaked the sheets. Huw had her pinned, her thighs high and her knees over his shoulders, unable to move even if she wanted to. From this commanding position, he began to thrust into her, long and slow at first.

"You bastard," Astrid hissed, right on the edge of another climax. "More."

She writhed in his hold, her whole world shrunk to the immense pleasure of his plunging cock. "Oh!" she cried again.

Huw liked this position as he could see as well as feel another climax take her without warning and tumble her over the edge into the place. Her orgasms felt almost simultaneous—one beginning before the last had ended. It was a place Huw planned to take her to often as it seemed to combine well with his discipline to make her more malleable.

Finally, Huw felt himself approaching the end of his own journey into ecstasy. He made his final, shattering thrusts, pressing his thumb down on Astrid's clit, shocking her pleasure centers into her own final, shuddering orgasm. They came together, Astrid's sheath tightening along his length as he emptied his balls into her.

They stayed there for a moment, suspended in time, their breathing ragged, as they slowly came back to their senses. Huw gently pulled out and wrapped her in his arms. She wriggled against him and smiled as she felt his cock respond. He'd never before had a woman who so inflamed him that he was barely finished with her before his cock started to harden again. He felt much like he had when he was a randy lad fucking anything female, but Astrid wasn't just any female. She was his woman, and he meant to claim her and bind her to him in all ways.

"I told you to take care lest you awaken the one-eyed beast. It's time you learn that more than your mouth or your cunt can take my staff. Hands and knees, Astrid."

"Why...what are you going to do?" she asked suspiciously.

"I suspect your elders taught you the answer to that. Has a man ever buried his cock balls deep in your dark passage?"

"N...no..."

He smiled. "Good. Then I shall claim it for my own. Hands and knees, Astrid, or it's back over my knee before you get on your hands and knees."

Astrid searched his face. Huw kept his expression

neutral but folded his brawny arms across his chest. He meant to show her there was more than one way to punish her bottom.

"Now...Astrid. I mean to punish your bottom from the inside. The worst part will be, as with the spanking, you will enjoy it."

"I don't enjoy being spanked..."

"And yet each time you become aroused and your pussy softens and gets wet in order to accommodate my cock. Hands and knees."

Astrid closed her eyes and took a deep breath, exhaling slowly, and then did as she was told.

"Lower your upper body and spread your legs. Present your ass to me for my pleasure."

"Huw..."

His hand snaked out and delivered a stinging swat to her bottom. Astrid yowled but did as he'd ordered.

"Good girl," he said. "I'm going to take this ass and make you like it."

He reached between her legs and scooped out some of her cum, slathering his cock and her puckered entrance with it. As he got her ready, he pressed against it until it gave way and he had a finger inside her. Gods if her pussy was tight, her asshole might well strangle his cock, but his cocked bobbed up and down, dripping pre-cum, desperate to breach her darkest hole. Huw rubbed the reddened cheeks of her ass, soothing her fears as he penetrated her again.

"Flatten your back, Astrid, don't you try to keep me out. This is mine," he said, fingering her up to his second knuckle, "and I mean to claim it as well."

Huw leaned down and kissed the small of her back as he removed his finger and placed the bulbous head of his cock against her dark rosette then pressed forward, gently forcing it wider as he pushed in, sliding past the tight ring of muscle. He fucked into her gently, letting her body direct when he pushed forward and when he pulled back. Inch by inch, he gained ground, allowing her to adjust but never giving up ground he'd already won.

He felt Astrid's absolute capitulation to his dominance when her body took on the languid quality he usually only saw when he'd fucked her thoroughly and filled her with his cum. He meant to fill her again...in a totally new place. Gods she felt incredible. She was too tight, and her ass now fought to keep him as he dragged backward with each thrust forward being easier.

"Huw," she purred—no distress in her tone.

Huw responded by building—too slowly, it was

torture--the speed and force of his thrusts, until Astrid was gasping with each one. Her sounds of pleasure further inflamed him, and Huw began to lose himself in the act of driving into her.

"That's right," he growled. "Take it. Love it."

He wasn't going to last long. His proud Witch of the Ironwood had submitted. Oh, he didn't expect that meant she would be a good girl all the time...in fact, he hoped she wouldn't. He rather enjoyed spanking her pretty bottom, but this felt just as good.

He groaned as a shiver went up his spine and he began to move inside her. Wanting her to enjoy this new pleasure, he slid his hand underneath and found her clit. It was slippery with her own juices, and he ground his thumb against it as he went balls deep, his cum gushing forward. She cried out in orgasm.

Astrid's ass clamped down on his staff. Her breathing was labored but pleasured. He filled her ass, fucking in and out with strong, sure strokes until he had emptied himself in her. He fell forward, catching himself on his powerful arms, nuzzling and kissing the back of her neck.

"Gods, yes!" Astrid sighed as she collapsed beneath him exhausted. His cock slipped from her ass as she lay totally spent beneath him.

He stroked her back and rose from the bed, taking a damp cloth to clean both himself and her before disposing of the cloth and joining her back in the bed, stretching out beside her, and spooning her against him as he closed his eyes and joined her in the land of dreams.

***

They were awakened the next morning by rapping on their door. “Up we get now!” came Guthrum’s voice from the hallway. “It’s time to see our man.”

“Sweet Frigga, is it still dark?” murmured Astrid sleepily as she began to stir.

Huw pushed his hair out of his eyes, and sat up. “Guthrum was always one for an early start.”

There was another rapping at the door again, more insistent this time.

“Don’t lose your feathers, you old crow!” shouted Huw. “We’re up, we’re up.”

“I’m sure you were up most of the night, Huw, but are you two separate entities or are you once again forming the hump-backed beast? Leave your witch alone and get downstairs. Hurry up, or there’s no food for you.”

They heard him stomp down the stairs, looked at each other, and laughed.

"You heard the man," said Huw, pulling on his trousers and his tunic. "Get a move on. He's not kidding about the food."

"Men," grumbled Astrid. "The whole idea of restorative sleep is a mystery to the lot of you."

"Maybe I find rest and recouperation in things other than sleep," Huw announced, smacking her lightly on the bottom.

In spite of herself, Astrid laughed. She rolled up on the bed and winced. She shot a look at Huw, who managed to hide his grin to a certain extent.

"It's not funny," she grumbled.

"No, my beautiful witch, but it will get better. You will be fine, if a little sore. Best you keep that in mind when next you think to use your feminine charms against me.

A few minutes later they were down in the main room. Guthrum, despite his threats, had hot bacon and roasted appleflesh waiting for them. It smelled delicious and tasted better.

"A good night's sleep, I hope?" Guthrum asked innocently. Huw and Astrid darted a glance at each other, and all three laughed.

"Is that why you woke us so early, old man? Jealous?" teased Huw.

Chuckling, Guthrum shook his head. “Nay, lad. But we must be up when the forges are lit, for it’s the blacksmith we’re going to see. Or rather, the blacksmith’s father.”

“He’s the one who knows about the *bengands*?” asked Astrid, scooping up more of the delicious mixture of bacon and apple.

“The very one.” Guthrum nodded then paused. “But we need to step carefully. The blacksmith is a decent fellow...but his father is not. As nasty a piece of work as I’ve seen. Best you not speak at all, dear lady, or even make him aware of your presence.”

Astrid felt a flash of anger. *Another man of the old type*. However, if he had the knowledge they needed, they would have to step carefully. She swallowed her anger. “Should I stay here?” she asked, keeping her voice carefully neutral.

Guthrum shook his head. “Nay. The old man is blind. Keeping your mouth shut and your ears open will suffice.”

Huw stole a glance at his companion, nodding when she held her tongue.

Good girl, he mouthed to her before saying, “Let’s go, old friend.”

Guthrum nodded and led them out into the

streets. Uppsala before dawn was quiet, but not entirely still. Those whose craft required them to be up in the early hours were already at work. Astrid could hear the quiet chatter of the bakers as they fired their ovens and began to prepare their bread. Novices from the temple complex were sweeping the entranceway which stood between two large wooden columns.

Finally, they came upon the reddish glow that emitted from the blacksmith's forge. The forge was covered by a timber roof, but otherwise open to the air. Astrid could feel the heat as they approached, and the blacksmith himself was shirtless save for a thick leather apron. Despite the cold morning air, he was already sweating, but seemed to notice neither the sweat nor the occasional spark which drifted from his anvil, where he was at work at the shaping of a large iron pan.

In a corner of the forge, close enough to feel the heat but not so close that it was smothering, sat an old man, one hand tightly wrapped around a drinking horn from which he occasionally sipped. Where his eyes should have been was a wrinkled mass of scar tissue. He tilted his head as the three approached, despite the noise of forge and hammer.

I'll have to step quietly and breathe softly,

thought Astrid, noting the keenness of the old man's hearing.

"We have visitors, Jan," called the old man to his son, in a cracked, gravelly voice.

The burly smith put down his hammer and turned to face the new arrivals. "It's the men I told you about, Father," he said with a warning glance at Astrid. "Old Guthrum the Jomsviking and his friend, Huw."

The old man cocked his head and frowned, but before he could say anything, Guthrum stepped forward. "Good to see you again, Sigismund," he said companionably. "My friend Huw is a Jomsviking like myself and seeks some of your lore. Huw, this is Sigismund, who was a master craftsman in his time."

"Well met, Sigismund," said Huw respectfully.

"I *was* a master craftsman, just as Guthrum *was* a great warrior," snapped Sigismund in a tone of malice. "I lost my craft when I lost my sight to the fire of Miklagard, which no water can quench. I wonder what Guthrum's excuse is?"

The old warrior's eyes narrowed, but he held his tongue. "Time and old age lay their hands on all men's shoulders, Sigismund."

"Save for those who are brave enough to spend their lives in war," said the blind craftsman, sipping at his cup.

Huw interjected hastily. “Master craftsman, I come seeking knowledge of the *bengands*.”

This was clearly novel enough to turn Sigismund from his accustomed bitter course. “The bone wands? Now there was a pretty piece of craft. Made to bring the pinchprick bitches of Ironwood to account.” He spat into the fire. “So, what would you wish to know about them?”

“Master Sigismund, what exactly do they do, and how do they do it?” Huw knew the old man would most likely would sour again soon, and hoped to gain as much as he could before it happened.

“You don’t ask much, do you?” asked Sigismund wryly, but the Astrid could tell he was proud of his work, and wanted to boast about it. “Made of walrus tusk and amber, with the runes of binding and unleashing held hidden by the priests of Uppsala. Designed for one purpose only: to bring the witches to ruin. The finest weapons of a proud order.”

“A proud order?” asked Huw.

The old man’s face twisted in a cruel smile. “Aye. The *Brennari*.”

It took all of Astrid’s self-control not to gasp in horror.

The *Brennari*. The Burners. The ultimate enemy of all witches, of Ironwood or anywhere else. Ruthless, cruel, and vindictive, the Burners had sought their goal with a terrifying single-minded obsession: to put every woman accused of witchcraft to the flame. The elder Sisters refused to talk about them, save to spit at the mention of their name.

Huw glanced at Guthrum, who looked back at him in alarm. “I...I thought the *Brennari* were long gone, Master Sigismund.”

Sigismund cackled with laughter and shook his head. “Brought low by the edicts of Jarls who feared their power. Their fire was dimmed but not extinguished. But as my son knows well, fire can hide to spring forth in the most surprising places. And as the dark crafts of Miklagard show us, not every fire can be extinguished,” he finished bitterly.

“So the *Brennari* crafted the bone wands?” prompted Huw.

The old man sat up straight. “With my help, they did. None save me had the skill to craft such mighty runes onto physical objects without splitting them asunder. Proud I was, to do it! I only wish the Burners had been able to wield them properly, to put every split-tail on a pyre and hear the bitches scream.”

Astrid shuddered. Although the vicious old man was blind, he had turned his head once again and seemed to be staring directly at her.

"What stopped them from using them properly?" asked Guthrum.

"Still here, *retired* warrior?" snapped Sigismund. Guthrum gripped his belt until his knuckles turned white, but waited him out.

"Four of the *bengands* were made," said the old man eventually. "So that the noble *Brennari* could fall upon the Ironwood from each of the four directions, and not a single split-tail could escape. The Brothers had almost managed to wipe them out once, you see, but some of the little worms fled the trap. This time, the obliteration was meant to be complete, from every crone to every twisted little she-bitch."

Astrid closed her eyes as she imagined the devastation these men intended to wreak. *By my life, this must not be allowed to come to pass*, she swore silently.

"So, there are four," said Huw heavily.

Sigismund nodded, tilting his head toward the broad-built warrior. "There's a question in that statement, or I'm a fool."

"Where are they?" asked Huw, carefully keeping

his voice neutral.

The old man kept them waiting as he sipped from his cup then smacked his wrinkled lips. "All four started here, in Uppsala. Made in secret and kept ready and waiting while the *Brennari* rebuilt in secret. The priests of Uppsala held them as relics of powerful magic, but did not know their true purpose. They believed they were merely magical counterbalances to the power of the Ironwood, to be held against their rising strength. The fools had no idea the bone wands were objects meant for destruction not protection. And then the damned idiots let one be stolen from their grasp." He spat into the fire once more.

"So, what happened then?" prompted Huw.

"It forced the Brothers into action, even though they were not fully ready!" replied Sigismund angrily. "The other three were given to the *Brennari* who were still mustering their forces for the slaughter. A Brother was sent to retrieve the one that had been stolen. The moment for attack was not yet ripe, but needs must." He shrugged.

"So who holds the remaining *bengands*?" pressed Huw.

Sigismund chuckled. "Enough. For you to be asking these questions, you must have obtained one of the wands. Show it to me."

Everyone stood silently, unsure what to do. Huw and Astrid looked at each other uncertainly.

"Come, come!" demanded Sigismund, gesturing. "I long to hold one of my creations once more, before death claims me at last."

Finally, Huw spoke. "It is not here, master craftsman."

The old man laughed contemptuously. "You think me a fool. I know you would not let it out of your sight, Huw of Hestur."

Huw stepped back in shock, and Sigismund laughed once more.

"You think me feeble-minded? Who else would come asking about the bone wands save the man who had stolen one and seized another? But you and your troll-dung bitch will find your end here."

Huw leapt to the side to avoid the lethal downward swing of a heavy hammer from behind him. He drew his long-knife from its sheath as he turned, and, before the blacksmith could recover, Huw stabbed the aproned figure in the belly and ripped upward. He stepped back as the blacksmith fell to the ground.

Sigismund laughed bitterly, not moving from his chair. "The boy was always a better smith than a fighter."

The three companions looked at him in shock and horror.

"But no mind. Others will be here soon enough, to finish the job he bungled," the old man said complacently.

Huw surged forward, seizing Sigismund by the throat and holding his still-bloody long-knife to the old man's flesh.

"How do we destroy them, you miserable wretch?" he snarled.

Sigismund merely laughed. "Do you really imagine death holds any fear for me? Do your worst, fighting man."

Huw cursed and shoved the old man back into his seat.

"To the right!" called Guthrum in warning. Sure enough, figures were emerging out of the early morning darkness, loping steadily toward them. The firelight from the forge flickered on their blades.

"Away from here, out of the light!" shouted Huw.

Astrid, who had been shocked into a kind of immobility, began to move, but Sigismund was not done. He reached out a gnarled hand and tripped her as she started to run. Astrid fell to the ground, reaching behind her—grasping for anything she might use as a weapon. The presence of the *bengand* meant her sorcery was of no use. As the old man used his hold on her ankle to crawl on top of her, she wrapped her hand around an iron rod. She recoiled in horror as she felt his stinking breath on her face.

"I knew you were there the whole time, she-bitch," he cackled. "Your sorcerous aura shines bright to those who know how to see, even a blind man. How does it feel to..."

Seizing the iron shaft, she pulled it from the forge. "How does *this* feel?" Astrid cut him off, hitting him with her makeshift weapon and then, realizing it was a brand, she thrust it into his wrinkled face. The smell of burning flesh assailed her nostrils and made the contents of her stomach roil. The old man fell away; Astrid got to her feet and looked around.

"Which way do we run?" she demanded.

"You two, on your way," said Guthrum grimly. "I'll never keep pace, and I feel my death-song rising within me."

"No!" protested Astrid, but Huw took her by the arm and led her away at a run.

"He's right, and he means to win his way into Valhalla with this fight. We cannot deny him his fate," said Huw forcefully.

Astrid sobbed as they ran, and turned back one more time to look at the old warrior. She prayed to Freyja to give him the strength and stamina he would need to have the Valkyries ride to take him to his final resting place...the hallowed halls of Valhalla. Guthrum shoved his axe into the fires of the forge, heating the blade as he waiting for the approaching attackers. He was laughing and singing as the battle joy took him.

When they turned the corner, they could see no more.

Chapter Ten

Huw sat morosely and stared down at the city below them from where they hid, tucked high among the hills above Uppsala. Astrid regarded the warrior uncertainly. The horror of what they had experienced in the forge lay heavy on them, and Astrid was also worried about how her companion was handling the loss of his old friend. Huw had said little since they had fled the town, making their way into the hills even as the first rays of dawn broke over them.

"Guthrum was a brave man," Astrid said softly, sitting next to Huw and putting her arm around his shoulder.

"Aye," said Huw gloomily. "He had a good death. It's what he wanted."

"His sacrifice saved us," said Astrid.

"It did." Huw paused. "I just...if it had been me alone, I would have stood with him. If it was meant to be my death, then I would have met it and laughed. But now? Now I run." He folded his arms across his chest.

"It was the right thing to do," said Astrid softly.

"We have a higher cause we need to stay alive to fight for."

"Don't I know it?" asked Huw angrily. "All I was thinking was to get the *bengand* out of there, that we couldn't let them have it. That we are the only ones standing between your Ironwood and slaughter. That we needed to stay alive to fight another day." He sighed. "I fear this quest has unmanned me."

"No," insisted Astrid, moving closer to him. "It has made you a better man. You are fighting for something greater than yourself."

Huw looked at her. "You truly think so?"

"I know so," said Astrid, and met his mouth with hers in a searing kiss.

She felt his arms encircle her in a powerful grasp, and let herself move further into him, abandoning her fear and worry and allowing her passion, her growing love for this man, take its place.

"My witch, my Astrid," he murmured as he kissed along her jawline.

She threw her head back, and Huw unbuttoned her tunic to bury his face between her breasts. With one hand, he circled one of her nipples, while his tongue played with the other. With his free hand, he cupped her bottom and pulled her into his lap.

Astrid lifted her skirt, and pressed her warm pussy against the bulge of his cock. Huw moaned slightly as he quickly moved to unfasten his trousers and release his cock.

"Yes," murmured Astrid as she slipped her hand down to press his shaft to the entrance of her core. Already she was wet and ready to receive him. Huw gripped her waist, moving her until her slick sheath was above his waiting cock. With a forceful downward motion, he impaled her on it.

Astrid gasped in shock and pleasure. He was so strong! He held her helpless in his grasp, completely in control of her body as he pumped her up and down the length of his cock. He moved her as if she weighed no more than a feather.

Astrid was being bounced delightfully up and down, the force of Huw's movements driving him deeper into her than he had ever gone before. Locked in his grip, she surrendered herself to his iron control, and threw her head back, losing herself to her first orgasm.

"Sweet goddess," she moaned as Huw continued his relentless motion, with no pause or interlude. Wave after wave of climaxes rushed through her body.

Up and down he pumped her, making her ride

him harder than she ever would have been capable. Just as it was starting to become too much, too overwhelming, Huw leaned his head forward into the abundance of her breasts. The rough bristling of his beard against the sensitive skin of her areolas drove her higher into pleasure, and she cried out in surprise and delight.

"Yes, Huw!" she cried, his hips beginning to rock back and forth, increasing the violence and intensity of their lovemaking.

Their bodies crashed together and Huw took her nipple between his teeth, nipping and tugging, his cock pounding her pussy ceaselessly. Astrid cried his name as Huw gave one final, massive surge and flooded her pussy with his cum. The inundation of his creamy essence into her ravaged pussy tipped her over the edge one final time, and Astrid heard Huw moan as her core shuddered, pulsing all along the length of his cock, drawing every last drop from him.

They stayed there, she on his lap, he inside her, holding each other close, their breathing slowing and returning to normal. Huw leaned his head into her chest, as she laid her cheek on the top of his head.

Finally, Huw looked up at her. "How did you become my everything, witch? If I didn't know better, I would say you had ensorcelled me."

Astrid cupped his face and kissed him, long and deeply. "I could ask the same thing of you, warrior. If you are my fate, then I thank all the gods and goddesses."

"Aye," Huw moved her gently off of him, and began to rearrange himself. Astrid did the same.

"But they have a price for their blessings. We have a task to complete."

"So we do," agreed Astrid. "But where does it take us next? Uppsala may have become too hot for us, at least at this moment."

"You're not wrong." Huw moved to pack up their things. "We dare not try to destroy this bloody bone wand until we can be sure that the act of destroying it will not consume us as a result. And there are three more to be found. At least we know who our enemy truly is now."

"The *Brennari,*" said Astrid, shuddering. "I have not seen them in my lifetime, but the few times the elder Sisters were willing to speak of them...they were terrible, Huw, truly terrible. So many women burned, innocents in the wrong place as well as my sisters."

"Cowards, the lot of them," said Huw shortly. He stopped, and turned to face his companion.

"Astrid, you must understand that Brynn and I knew nothing of this when we stole a *bengand* from the priests of Uppsala. We thought it a tool to help Brynn avenge the insult committed by Kasia and claim her as his own. We had no idea what was truly intended with these awful things."

Astrid nodded. "I know. There remains the issue of why you thought it necessary to bring your mischief to the Ironwood, and we will have to reckon with this, but it pales in comparison with what we know now. You are not the man to commit such horrors as the Burners plan, Huw, and I know it."

Huw exhaled. "I'm glad. What these men seek to do...it's unholy. It's against the gods, and especially the goddesses. Such hatred!" He shook his head. "It's a sickness."

Astrid stopped what she was doing to go over to Huw and embrace him. "I can't tell you how happy it makes me that you see things that way. When we face such madness, it's good to know who can be counted upon."

Huw kissed the top of her head. "Aye. And fortunately, I have an idea for what we do next."

Astrid looked up at him. "Truly?" she asked, excitedly.

Huw nodded. "Just as there are men who would never take part in such a thing, there are men who would." His face darkened. "And I know one of them. If the *Brennari* are still a force, as they clearly are, he's a man to know about it."

"And he will share this with us?" asked Astrid, frowning.

Huw smiled wolfishly. "He will when I'm finished asking him."

***

A few days' journey brought them once again to the coast, looking down from the hills onto a fisherman's cottage, close to the open water. An old jetty stuck out into the water, fish and eel traps in a tangled mess at its end. It was once again near dawn, and Astrid could feel the cold in the air. Fall was coming, and the air was beginning to turn chill.

"Doesn't look like much," she said.

"Bjarni has good reason to keep a low profile." Huw chuckled. "He was a turncoat the last time raiders struck Visby. He tipped them off to when the fighting men were gone and collected a chest of silver for his pains. He was found out, however, and the people of Visby were howling for his blood. He thought it best to take his silver and leave. A coward, but a rich coward.

One who wishes to be left well enough alone." Huw smiled. "But he will not get his wish this day."

As they watched, the cottage door opened, and a man of middle years emerged. A shambling mess of furs and rags, he stumbled down the jetty and stopped to urinate into the water.

"Enjoy the drink, Njord!" called the man. "Let me know if you have any complaints."

Huw shook his head. "It's a foolish man who taunts the gods," he murmured. "Come on," he said to Astrid, "let's bring him a message from Njord." His teeth flashed white, and he got up from the brush to stride down to the jetty. Astrid followed at his heels.

"Bjarni, old man!" bellowed Huw. The man turned and dropped the trap he was carrying, his mouth wide open in shock. "Don't you know it's dangerous to taunt the gods?" Huw laughed, loudly and threateningly. "They might just send...well, me." He stood at the landward end of the jetty, his feet planted wide.

Bjarni looked rapidly to his right and left, but there was nowhere to go, unless he wanted to swim. There was no escape and the old man smiled in welcome, revealing a mouth of rotten teeth.

"Huw of Hestur! By Odin's beard, it's been years! So good to see you! And you've brought a friend."

Bjarni strode forward to embrace Huw, but stopped when Huw raised a warning hand.

"That's close enough, Bjarni. Do you think I've forgotten who you are?"

Bjarni's face turned sullen. "Ah, that old gossip, Huw," he whined. "How long must a man live that down."

"That depends on what the man did," replied Huw. "I wonder what the good citizens of Visby would say to that?"

Fear and resentment flashed across Bjarni's face, before he replaced them with an ingratiating smile. "Ah, but you're not from Visby, are you? You're welcome to all the hospitality I can offer. You and your little friend."

"It's not hospitality I'm looking for, Bjarni. I'm looking for information."

Bjarni spread his arms and bowed slightly, rocking on his heels. "I would of course be happy to help an old friend. What do you wish to know?"

"About the *Brennari*."

Bjarni's eyes flashed toward his cottage for a brief moment, then back to Huw. "Long gone, friend. Nothing but stories, now."

"Astrid," Huw said calmly, "go search this fine

man's cottage, while I have a closer word with him."

Bjarni tried to dart past Huw to get to land, but Huw seized him in an iron grip and marched the protesting man to the end of the jetty. "Go on, Astrid. I'll deal with this fellow," he called over his shoulder.

Astrid nodded and cautiously opened the door to the cottage, quickly peering inside before she entered. There was no one within. Astrid wrinkled her nose. The place had an overwhelming stink of fish and sweat. There was little to look at—a chair, a bed, a hearth—but she did notice a small lockbox tucked beneath his malodorous mattress.

Pulling it out, she examined the lock. Not too complex. She muttered under her breath, and the lock sprang open.

From outside, she heard the sound of a splash, and Bjarni's loud voice of complaint. Astrid smiled, and opened the box. Inside was a piece of vellum parchment, a rare thing, and totally out of place in this wretched dwelling. She picked it up and stood next to the door, to let the light fall upon it.

The parchment had been inscribed with runes, which Astrid recognized and was able to read. On the sheet was a list of names and dates. She recognized some of the names as prominent towns and landholdings, but others were unknown to her.

With the list in hand, Astrid left the cottage, only to be met by Huw, who was leaving the jetty.

"Were you able to find anything?" he asked.

"Look at this," said Astrid, holding up the parchment.

Huw glanced at it and said sheepishly, "Not all the runes here are familiar to me. Are you able to read what it says?"

"I think so," she replied. "I don't know all of these words, but what I recognize seem to make up a list of towns and holdings, with dates next to them."

Huw nodded. "That runs an even course with what I learned from Bjarni. He seems to have been a coordinator for the Burners, receiving and passing along messages, as well as sums of coin. What is the closest place and date, by your reckoning?"

Astrid peered over the list once more. "A landholding not far from here, just a little farther down the coast. The date listed next to it is two days from now. We should be able to make it in a day, if we move quickly."

"Then let that be our next target, and we'll see what we can see," said Huw.

"Where is Bjarni?" asked Astrid.

Huw smiled grimly. "The citizens of Visby have had their justice."

Astrid nodded.

***

A day's journey saw them camped on a ridge, overlooking a modest hall and outbuildings.

"Doesn't seem like a place for a conspiracy," Astrid observed, regarding the holding below.

"Who knows what ill may be planned, even in a place such as this?" asked Huw rhetorically.

"Room enough for all manner of mischief. Who is to mark the comings and goings of such a remote hall? Let's observe what traffic the day brings."

The two found a closer spot from which to observe the hall, and, sure enough, they noted three separate travelers arrive and make their stay within the thatch-roofed hall.

"A little busy for an average day," said Astrid.

"It does indeed look like mischief is afoot," nodded Huw. "When night falls, I'll make my way down, and see what passes. You stay here and wait for me."

"Wait for you?" repeated Astrid, stung. "What do you mean, wait for you? An extra set of hands may come in useful."

Huw turned from his observation to look at her. "Which of us knows battle? Not you, I think. I won't have you poking your head needlessly into danger."

"While it's fine for you?" demanded Astrid.

"I make my living putting myself into danger. Leave the fight to those who are used to risking their skins, woman," replied Huw, his tone a little too condescending for Astrid's liking.

"To the Norns with that idea!" she said, stung. "Haven't I risked my skin enough to prove my worth?"

"Listen to me, my witch," replied Huw, "I'll not worry about any skin but my own down there. You'd best mind me, or you'll pay the price for it. Have you forgotten so soon what it is to have a red bottom?"

"Have you forgotten that we are both on this quest together?" Astrid retorted.

"Look at me. No, look me in the eyes!" Huw leveled his gaze at her, and she looked defiantly back. "This is my decision, and it is final. You move one step from this place before I tell you, and you'll end up facedown over my knee, and soon regret it. Do you understand?"

His expression and tone of voice was so fierce Astrid gave way. "Yes, I understand," she murmured.

"Good." Huw turned to resume his observation of

the hall. “Then let that be an end to it.”

Whatever you say, fighting man, she thought sarcastically, but was wise enough not to say it out loud.

The two remained watching in silence, as the day passed into evening, but there were no more visitors. As the first stars could be seen in the night sky, Huw stood up and said, “Now is the time. I will go to see what there is to be seen. And what will you be doing?”

“Staying here until you say otherwise,” replied Astrid dutifully.

“Good girl.”

Huw stepped into the night and was soon gone from view.

Astrid waited what seemed to her to be a reasonable amount of time then muttered, “And if you believed that, you’re a fool, big man,” and made her way in the darkness toward the lights of the hall.

Out of caution—as much in fear of Huw as if any stranger—Astrid used her powers to ensure she moved silently in the night. She did not have the craft to render herself invisible, but she could make herself as stealthy as any woodland creature. She passed quickly and quietly through the woods next to the path that led to the hall, and soon saw the furtive figure of Huw himself, moving from hayrick to barn, as he crept up to the hall itself.

Astrid kept a healthy distance from the warrior, who moved with astonishing lightness for one so large. *He knows what he's about, that's for certain*, thought Astrid as she watched, half in admiration. *I would not want him stalking me. It's a good thing he's not looking behind himself*! Caught by the notion, she quickly looked back, but there was no one on her trail.

In the moment she looked back, she lost track of Huw. *Where has he gone?* she wondered, until a slight movement on the roof showed him moving slowly across the thatch, toward the smoke-hole positioned above the hearth within the hall.

***

Huw crept stealthily along the thatched rooftop, carefully keeping his weight spread so that there was no telltale dip in the roof for those below to see. He inched his way up until he was next to the smoke-hole above the hearth. Despite the occasional plumes of smoke, he could see into the hall below easily enough.

Four figures gathered around the hearth, talking. By their body language, he guessed that they were not all closely familiar with one another. They spoke in frustratingly low tones, and he could not make out what they were saying. He did his best to survey the entirety of the hall, but he could see no one else. Whatever their business, they were keeping it close.

Finally, one of the men stood up and pulled a satchel off his shoulder. Huw held his breath. *Come on, let's see it, you bastard.* Sure enough, the man pulled out an ivory walrus tusk almost identical to the one Huw carried. The conversation between the men below suddenly increased in intensity.

Good enough for me. Time to even up the score for Guthrum. He levered his body up and swung nimbly down into the hall, aiming his jump to avoid the burning hearth.

"Hello lads." He smiled wolfishly and drew his sword.

With one swift stroke, Huw had one man down, holding his stomach. Two others hastily drew their swords, but the man with the bone wand turned and fled toward the door to the hall.

Loki's balls! Huw swore inwardly, even as he slammed his shoulder into the nearest man, sending him flying. Another swung an overhand stroke at Huw's head, but he seized the man's wrist, head-butted him, and tossed him aside. The man with the bone wand was almost at the door.

One man was down, one getting up, and the third fighter seemed to have been knocked unconscious. Huw snapped his arm forward, and a dagger flew from his hand to catch the second man in the throat. "I'm not done with you yet, lad!" he snarled as he ran in pursuit of the fourth.

However, the last man had already opened the door of the hall and was preparing to flee into the night when he suddenly startled backward, throwing an arm in front of his face. A moment was all Huw needed to slam the hilt of his sword into the back of the man's head, dropping him.

At the open door stood Astrid, pale-faced.

"I...I tried to cast a spell on him, but it didn't work!" she said, appearing shocked and confused.

"Of course, it bloody didn't," replied Huw angrily. "He carries a *bengand*. I told you to stay back!"

"I thought you'd need my help, you big ox!" Astrid shot back.

"Well for Odin's sake, don't you move now!" Huw checked over the scene. Two men were dead, and two were unconscious. He quickly found rope and tied the two unconscious men up tightly, securing them both to different hall posts so that even if they woke, they could not move. He shoved the *bengand* into his satchel, where it met the other with a clatter of bone.

He looked over the hall once more and nodded. "And now, girl," he said to Astrid as he took her arm in a firm grip, "we're off to the barn for a chat, you and I."

Astrid struggled and protested but could not shake Huw's grip as he marched her to the holding's small barn. With one hand, he pulled the door back. The barn was empty. Huw stepped inside and sat down on a hay bale, dragged Astrid across his hard thighs, and trapped her lower body by looping one leg over hers. In a trice, he had Astrid's backside bared, despite her squirms and struggles.

Smack! His hand came down on her bare ass, causing Asrtid to yelp. "I warned you, Astrid, did I not?"

Smack! "I thought you'd need help!" she wailed.

Smack! *Smack*! "And yet I told you clearly that I would not," said Huw calmly as he continued to punish her. Her shapely ass was already beginning to pinken as she struggled. He continued to spank her with a steady rhythm, making sure to cover every inch of her gorgeous bottom. "We knew there was likely a bone wand there that would render your magic useless, and you as helpless as a newborn babe."

"I just wanted to help you! Ow ow ow! I did not

want to see you come to harm! Ouch! I *love* you, you big oaf!"

Abruptly, Huw stopped, his hand resting on her heated bottom. "What did you say?" he asked, startled.

Her tears flowed. "I love you," she answered, no longer shouting. "If you were to be hurt, I would die inside."

Huw was gently stroking her ass, soothing the heat with his fingers. "Oh, my witch," he breathed, "I love you too. Why do you think I wanted you to stay behind? I would never see you come to harm."

Astrid turned to look up at him, from her position over his knee. "Then let me up, you ox, and let me kiss you."

Huw did not slacken his grip but simply shook his head. "A promise is a promise, my beloved witch. Your spanking is not done. Perhaps this will make you think twice before disobeying me again."

"What?" Astrid shrieked in outrage then yowled as he resumed her discipline.

She kicked her feet and tried to rise, but to no avail. He held her in place as he rained blow after blow across her backside, reigniting and increasing the fire he had left just moments before.

"Please!" she pleaded, but he continued without

pause.

She continued to fight. The harder she did, the harder the slaps to her ass. Finally, after all her struggles failed to win her any advantage or pause, her body relaxed into his. She slumped over his knee, truly accepting her punishment, his right to inflict it upon her, and his dominance. Huw continued for a while longer, to truly reinforce the importance of obeying him, and then paused, resting his hand once again upon her ass, which was radiating heat.

"Astrid," said Huw, "do you understand why it is important to obey my orders?"

"Y-yes," replied Astrid, between sobs.

Huw pulled her up and onto his lap, letting her lean into his chest, one hand rubbing her tender bottom. She looked up at him.

"Huw, I didn't just say it because I was over your knee." She brushed a tear from her cheek. "I love you, Huw of Hestur."

"Oh, my witch," he replied gently. "I love you, Astrid of the Ironwood, but you must submit to me."

He leaned his head down and took her mouth with his. They lost themselves to the kiss, exploring each other as they reveled in their passionate embrace. They continued to kiss, removing their clothes, falling to the floor of the barn and touching each other, Astrid's hands moving across Huw's broad chest, Huw palming her breasts and tweaking her nipples.

Their breathing grew quicker. Huw parted her legs, making a place for himself. His cock found the entrance to her core and he thrust inside.. She was on her back, Huw above her, propped on his powerful arms, both gazing into each other's eyes as he began his plunging rhythm.

"Sweet Freyja," murmured Astrid, gazing at him and smiling. "You feel so good."

Huw grinned, increasing the intensity of his thrusts, his cock pounding to the depths of her. He put his lips to her ear, tugging and nipping at her earlobe, before whispering, "You're mine, Astrid. I claim you."

She closed her eyes as he moved his mouth to her breasts, gently teething and tugging at her nipples. She arched her back--the first climax rushing over her. She gripped him tightly, as he continued his persistent pounding of her pussy.

"Mine, little witch. To do with as I please," Huw slammed into her.

"Yes, Huw! Yes! I am yours, take me!" she cried.

Her surrender was music to his ears as he pounded out the tempo of their passion. Huw knew the floor or the barn had to be hard against what had to be her tender bottom, but that knowledge only made everything even better, rawer, as she was ridden into ecstasy.

Huw flung her legs up, her knees crooked over his powerful shoulders, changing the angle of his thrusts to penetrate her more deeply. She cried his name again, spurring his motions to become more frenzied, driving inexorably toward his own explosive conclusion.

His roar mingled with her final cry as they reached their final peak together, his cock shooting ropes of thick cum into her, her pussy spasming along his length, drawing forth every last drop of his essence.

They lay there, Astrid on her back, Huw supported by the thick pillars of his arms above her, gazing at each other, their breathing steadily slowing. They smiled at each other.

"I cannot...I cannot say that I like being punished, Huw," said Astrid, recovering her breath, "but if every punishment were to end this way, I daresay I could get used to it."

"I doubt I could hold myself back from this, even if I wanted to," replied Huw, looking down at her. "But that's rather the point, my love. A punishment is meant to be an end of something, giving us leave to move on from it."

"I like it when you call me your love," Astrid purred happily.

"I like saying it, dear Astrid," said Huw. "I plan to say it for quite some time."

They shared a further moment, the heat of their bodies mingling, simply gazing at each other.

Then Huw sighed. "Sadly, the world waits for us." He kissed her deeply, one last time, then stood up and put on his clothes. He put a hand down to pull Astrid up, and she joined him.

"What should we do with the two you captured?" asked Astrid.

"We have what we came for," said Huw, "but if they are willing to trade knowledge for their lives, I will allow it."

The two companions returned to the hall, where both men still sat, tied to different hall posts. One looked at them when they entered, while the other—the one Huw had head-butted—still appeared to be unconscious. Huw walked to within a short distance of the man who had carried the *bengand* and had tried to flee, and squatted down.

"Do you know who I am?" he asked the bound

man.

"Sure, I do. Eirik told us all about you, and that bitch behind you. You're Huw of Hestur, and the split-tail is Astrid of the Ironwood."

Huw's expression did not change, but the blow he struck across the man's face was heavy.

"Mind your tongue, fellow, or you'll lose it. And what is your name?"

"My name is *Brennari*," the man spat back, eyes blazing with defiance. "A proud Brother of my Order. I have no other name."

Huw looked at him and nodded then straightened. "Well, let's see if your friend feels the same way."

He walked over to where the other man lay unconscious, picking up a horn of ale along the way. Huw dashed the ale in the man's face, bringing him to spluttering wakefulness.

Despite the fact he was now awake, the man did not look well. Huw's head-butt had clearly injured him severely. *He might even have a crack in his skull.* The fellow was muttering in a low tone and did not seem to be aware of his surroundings.

He leaned in close and whispered, "Brother! Brother, can you hear me? Are you all right?"

"Must get...must get to...take them all..." moaned

the man, his eyes glazed and unfocused.

"Where must we take them? Where, brother?" pressed Huw.

"The Mountain Crown...all four must meet at the Mountain Crown..."

"Sweyn! Shut your trap, you fool! He is not one of us!" called the other bound man. Astrid cursed, and looked for a cloth to gag him.

"The burning times begin at the Mountain Crown," said the head-butted man, his eyes and voice returned to clarity for a moment. He looked at Huw in confusion. "Who are you? I do not know your face..." he murmured, his eyes glazed over once again.

Huw straightened up. "No, Sweyn," he said, "You are a coward and a would-be murderer of helpless woman and children, just like your friend here. For the two of you, the burning times start now."

Huw and Astrid ignored the curses and cries as they walked out of the hall. As Huw stood a distance away with the two bone wands in his satchel, Astrid turned to face the hall.

"Take this, from a witch you couldn't burn," she said fiercely, and used her witchfire to light the thatched roof.

Neither she nor Huw said anything as they turned

away, the flames of the burning hall and the cries of the men following them into the night.

Chapter Eleven

The next morning, Huw stoked the fire he had kept burning low throughout the night. He had left Astrid's warm, sleeping embrace to make them some breakfast. He rubbed his hands together; the seasons were definitely turning, and the morning cold lasted longer each day.

Astrid rose sleepily and ran her hands through her hair. "No fear, my witch. You look as beautiful as always."

She laughed as she smoothed her hair down and ran a comb through it. "You might very well think so, mighty warrior, but you're biased."

"That I am." Huw took her up in a sweeping embrace, and kissed her deeply. Astrid surrendered to his kiss then, after a time, patted his chest.

"Breakfast, my lord. I'm starving," she teased.

"And I'm hungrier than I thought." Huw chuckled and returned to the fire. "We'll need more food before we go much farther," he said, examining their supplies. "I've no bow, but I can set some snares. Perhaps this evening, after we've traveled a spell.

"You sounded as if you recognized this place...the Mountain Crown?" asked Astrid as she took a seat on a nearby fallen tree.

Huw nodded. "Aye. An old hideout for bandits, raiders, and rogues. High up in the mountains, as the name implies. Haven't heard of anyone living there for years."

"Is it far? Should we look to get horses?"

"Nay," replied Huw. "From what I remember, it's tricky enough to reach on foot. Horses would have no chance."

"From what you remember?" teased Astrid. "When were you there? And which one were you? A bandit, a raider, or a rogue?"

Huw laughed. "We all find ourselves in a spot of bother from time to time, and need to lay low. 'Twas years ago, when I was just a young pup being foolish, and things got a little too hot."

"There's so much I don't know about you," said Astrid.

"Likewise, my witch, but there's not much to fill a saga in my life." He trimmed some stiff branches and notched them to form a tripod above the fire. "I was a terrible fisherman and a worse farmer when I was young, so I was no use to anyone. I fell in with some rough company and learned a sterner trade."

He carefully hung a pot from the tripod, and left it a short distance over the heat. Soon, a delicious smell arose from the stew within. Huw sighed as he poked the fire.

"Turns out I had found something I was truly good at. I was handy—more than handy—with blade and bow, and soon learned the difference between those who had courage and those who were full of wind. There are more of the latter than you might think! I wanted to fight in the company of those whom I could rely on to fight beside me. So, I went to Jomsburg."

This was more than Huw had ever offered of his past. He hoped Astrid could see it as a gift he had not given to others.

"A legendary place, by all accounts," she prompted.

Huw snorted. "That it was, and I look back and think myself more lucky than skilled to have survived the day of my joining. Less than twenty years old, I was! There's only one way to join the company. Did you know that?"

Astrid nodded. "You told me. By filling the boots of a Jomsviking, whom you've slain in single combat."

"Aye. I was a kid, full of piss and vinegar, but too

ignorant to know how outclassed I should have been." Huw breathed out, a rueful grin on his face. "The warrior who came out that morning to fight me was Hlithskjalf. I still remember his name. An absolute brute of a man! I near pissed myself when he marched out of the Burg. Fortunately for me, he had gone on a rampaging drunk the night before, and was slow and unsteady. He paid for it! I still raise a cup to him every Harvest Festival. They say you never forget the man whose boots you filled." Huw looked off into the distance for a brief moment, lost in memory, then turned his attention back to his stew. "Almost hot enough. So, what about you, my love? Where did you begin?"

Astrid flushed with pleasure at his intimate form of address. "I was born to the Ironwood," she said. "The daughter of a Witch of the Ironwood. I never knew which one. I was claimed and raised by the Sisterhood. A good upbringing. Some of the elder Sisters could be a bit terrifying to a young girl, and there's no such thing as perfect harmony, of course, but I grew up in the company of women who loved me and taught me everything I could learn and then some."

"So did you never know the company of men?"

asked Huw, curious.

It was Astrid's turn to laugh. "We knew enough! The physical differences were taught early, just as a matter of fact. As we came to womanhood, we were taught other things. As to the basic nature of men, well, the world taught us that."

"That is not true of all—" Huw began, but Astrid interrupted.

"Not all, Huw, but enough."

Huw could do nothing but nod in silent agreement. Astrid was right.

"So…my friend Brynn…" he ventured.

Astrid laughed. "It is an old magic," she said. "The elder Sisters have the knowledge of a spell that matches a witch who has come to womanhood with a man who is willing and viable. They bring him to the Ironwood for a night, long enough for the two to mate. The child of that union becomes a ward of the Ironwood. If the child is male, he is set up in an apprenticeship; there are plenty of families nearby who long for a strong son. If the child is female, she is raised as one of our own."

"So, the man is summoned whether he wills it or no?"

Astrid nodded. "In our experience, the men who

do not wish to join with a young and willing witch are few and far between."

Huw snorted. "In truth, I cannot recall Brynn ever complaining about what happened that night, only the manner of it."

Astrid smiled. "I have never heard Kasia complain either."

"I warn you now, my witch, that should Brynn recover, he will claim Kasia as his own, and you will not intervene." He held up his hand to stave off an argument. "So, is that what happened to the two of us? Did the elder Sisters match us together?"

Astrid shook her head. "No. In truth, none of the elder Sisters fully know what happened with you and I," she admitted. "I suspect the most wise see the direct hand of Freyja."

Huw let out a breath. "Odin's beard," he muttered. "That tallies with the strange experiences that I have had since all of us this began, but still, the whole matter is larger than my mind can span."

"I agree," said Astrid. "Knowing what we know now, it seems the threat to our Sisters is so great that Freyja herself has chosen to intervene."

"I wish she would tell us how to destroy the bloody things," said Huw.

"My thought is to send them to the bottom of the ocean," offered Astrid.

"As good a plan as any," he said. "Worth a try, when we find ourselves upon the waves again."

***

The two companions spent the day traveling through the forests of the foothills, steadily moving toward the mountain range that was their goal. Huw set a vigorous pace, eating up the miles with his steady strides, and Astrid was put to the test to keep up. However, she was a young and vigorous woman, with strength and determination, and she was not going to allow herself to fall behind. As the sun began to sink into the afternoon, Huw called a halt, and Astrid sighed inwardly with relief.

"If we want to eat past tomorrow, we'll need fresh game," announced Huw, setting down his pack. "I'll set snares down by the stream and check them in the morning. You, my witch," he said sternly, pointing a finger in warning, "will stay here, and not leave the campsite. If you move from here, you will spend time over my knee and not for your pleasure. Do you understand me?"

"I'm just supposed to sit here on my bottom while you range about the woods?" Astrid protested.

"If you want to be able to sit at all, then, yes," Huw replied shortly. "I'm warning you, Astrid, disobey me at your peril. I will not be as lenient as I have been."

He pulled his snares from his pack, and, with a last warning look back at Astrid, he loped off into the forest, toward the stream.

"Hmph," sniffed Astrid. "Not all men, my foot."

She wandered aimlessly around the campsite for a bit, before something caught her eye.

"Mushrooms!" she said happily, noting the presence of a ring of chanterelles, which she knew from experience to be delicious. The elder Sisters taught all the young witches in herb and plant lore, and Astrid almost salivated at the thought of the tasty addition the chanterelle mushrooms would bring to a stew. Besides, it would be nice to make a contribution. Huw was out getting food; she wanted to do her part.

As she carefully looked for and picked more mushrooms, Astrid lost sense of time and distance, focused entirely on her task. It was only when she straightened from her mushroom hunt and looked around that she realized two things: the sun was setting, and she had lost track of where the campsite was.

"Dammit," she muttered. "I'd better get back to

camp before he does, or Huw will blister my bottom."

After a few attempts to find familiar landmarks, Astrid gave up on forest craft and muttered an incantation for true finding. The spell gave her a sense of proper direction, and she rushed through the trees to reach the campsite. She caught her breath as she jogged into the clearing, only to see Huw sitting on a fallen log. His arms were crossed over his broad chest, and he shook his head as he glared at her.

"It's like my words pass right through your head, woman," he growled.

"I wasn't gone far!" protested Astrid, showing him the results of her search. "I noticed some mushrooms and thought they would make a nice addition to our stew. I was trying to help!"

"Astrid. What were the instructions I gave you?" asked Huw.

"I wasn't gone very long!" wailed Astrid.

"That wasn't what I asked. Answer my question...what were the instructions I gave you?"

Astrid bowed her head. "You told me not to move one step outside of the campsite."

He nodded. "Do you remember what I said would happen if you did?"

"You said you would put me over your knee," muttered Astrid.

"What was that?" said Huw sternly.

"You said you were going to put me over your knee!" said Astrid, more loudly. "But Huw, I was..."

"That's enough, my witch," Huw patted his lap. "Come here."

"No, Huw!" Astrid shook her head vigorously.

"Astrid," said Huw gravely, "if I have to get up and drag you over here, it will be my belt that you feel on your bare bottom."

Astrid stamped her foot on the ground in frustration. Huw simply looked at her, holding his hand up to beckon her. With an angry flounce, Astrid stomped over to the waiting Huw, and laid herself across his lap.

"Good girl," he murmured as he rucked her skirt up and bared her ass, leaving it vulnerable to his touch... and discipline.

He ran a hand over her buttocks in appreciation. Astrid shivered under his touch.

"You're going to learn to mind me, Astrid," began Huw, resting his hand on her bottom. "Why don't you tell me why you are here, facedown over my knee?"

"Because you won't listen to me," said Astrid

sullenly then yelped as Huw brought his hand down sharply twice, making her bottom dance.

"Try again," said Huw with a warning note in his voice.

"Because you told me not to leave the campsite, and I did," said Astrid, her tone still defiant.

Huw brought his hand down twice more, making her squirm.

"I wouldn't take that tone with me, if I were you, my witch," he said. "It tells me your ability to learn a lesson is still a long way off."

Huw spanked her thoroughly, bringing his hand down in a steady rhythm across both of her bottom cheeks. He paused for one brief moment to dip his hand between her thighs and chuckled, before trailing his finger up between the cleft of her ass cheeks to finger her puckered entrance, causing Astrid to struggle anew. Huw removed his finger and began to spank her again.

"It seems firm discipline agrees with you, Astrid." He continued the steady work of reddening her bottom.

"Not fair!" Astrid cried.

"It is nothing but fair. You were told to stay where I told you and chose to disobey," said Huw, bringing his hand down sharply yet again and again, heedless of Astrid's attempts to wriggle out of his grasp. "That choice is what concerns me. Your unwillingness to accept that you obey my commands or get your pretty bottom spanked."

"Who put you in charge?" demanded Astrid, then yelped yet again.

Huw chuckled again. "I would invite you to consider, my witch, which one of us is giving, and which one of us is receiving, a sound spanking," he observed, without pausing in his steady discipline.

Finally, Astrid submitted and accept Huw's punishment. He continued the spanking for a brief while longer then paused, gently running his fingers across her bottom.

"Astrid, do you understand that I expect you to obey my commands, even if you disagree with them, or don't understand them?" he asked.

"Yes, sir," answered Astrid, sniffling.

"I'm trying to keep you safe, Astrid. I love you and would sooner lose my arm than see harm come to you."

"I understand, sir. I...I love you, too."

"That's my good girl," said Huw soothingly, lifting her up and placing her in his lap. He began stroking her hair.

"I didn't set out to disobey you, you know," said Astrid, snug against his chest. "I just got distracted. I was trying to provide something for us...you've been the one doing everything."

"I know, Astrid, I know," murmured Huw, continuing to stroke her hair, and running a soothing hand over her tender bottom. "But providing for you is part of my responsibilities, and you can't scare me like that. Imagine how I felt when I walked into the campsite and found you gone!"

"Surely, Huw, there is some way I can make it up to you," said Astrid, running a finger down his chest toward his groin.

Huw gave a rumbling laugh from deep in his chest, mixing amusement and desire. "I see that what my fingers discovered did not lie."

"What can I tell you, mighty warrior?" asked Astrid, sliding off his lap and going to her knees in front of him. "I don't know why I even try to fight it." She pushed her hair back and tugged at his trousers. "Your mastery...does things to me."

Huw got to his feet, his cock springing loose and standing rock hard. "Does it indeed, my witch," he murmured, running his hands through her hair, and groaning as Astrid took him fully in her mouth, sliding her lips along his length before kissing the tip, then running her tongue from the tip to his balls.

"That's my good girl," Huw murmured, groaning once again as Astrid tightened her fingers in a circle at the base of his cock before working her mouth back and forth. "Gods!" he said through gritted teeth.

Astrid smiled as she looked up at him, then her eyes widened as Huw reached down, picked her up as if she weighed no more than a feather, and bent her over the fallen log he had been sitting upon moments ago.

"Oh, Huw!" cried Astrid in surprise, then gasped in pleasure as Huw, with barely a hesitation, took full advantage of her new position and thrust his cock into her pussy, taking her ferociously from behind.

The sheer force of his claiming made Astrid take a firm a grip on the log, giving a small moan of pleasure with every one of Huw's thrusts. Her noises of arousal and gratification seemed to drive Huw to even further frenzy, and Astrid wailed, a different note this time, as the first of her climaxes crashed over her.

"Sweet Freyja!" she cried, a second climax rocking her body mere moments after the first.

The sting of his body ramming into her tender

bottom only added more fuel to the fire, mixing the pleasure-pain sting into the waves of pleasure his vigorous stroking was giving her.

Huw seized her hips and pulled Astrid back a small space from the log, placing her hands on the fallen tree. Astrid looked back questioningly then cried out in pleasure as Huw reached around to take her swollen clit between his thumb and finger, rolling and tugging. Her knees buckled, another orgasm surging through her. Huw kept her hips in an iron grip, his cock seeking her soft entrance once again, thrusting into her even as his fingers kept circling and teasing at her clit.

Astrid cried his name again. The combination of his thrusting cock and his circling fingers brought her past any semblance of awareness, of knowing anything beyond his cock pumping her sheath and the waves of pleasure coming from her swollen nub.

Huw grunted and shifted his position slightly, increasing the frenzy of his thrusts, building toward his own release. Astrid thought in a flash she could not possibly climax again, nevertheless, his ruthless driving brought her crashing over the top one final time. Huw spasmed, sending his creamy essence to the very end of her sheath.

Huw remained inside her, breathing like he had just finished a race, his moan signaling his enjoyment of her pussy spasming a last few times. Finally, he withdrew, helping Astrid to stand up on wobbly legs, and they both reassembled their clothing and sat down on the log, Astrid wincing as her tender bottom rested on the rough bark.

She leaned her head against Huw's shoulder, sighing and basking in the warm afterglow. They sat companionably in silence for some brief moments, Huw wrapped his arm around Astrid, stroking her hair with his hand.

"I am sorry, Huw," said Astrid in genuine contrition, her hand on Huw's massive chest. "I hadn't even thought of what it must have felt like to walk into the camp and not see me there."

"I've had my say, you've had your punishment, and that's an end to it, my witch," said Huw soothingly. "I will admit my heart skipped a beat, but that's in the past now. I just want to keep you safe, Astrid," he continued earnestly. "I don't know what I'd do if I saw you harmed."

"I understand, my warrior," replied Astrid. "I feel the same fears. How can you expect me to sit by and watch while you risk your life?" She said it lightly, not wanting to start an argument.

“Look at me, Astrid.”

She tilted her face upward.

“Hear my voice, and understand. I am a warrior, one of the very best. Risking my skin is what I do. But know this: now that I have you to return to, nothing—not even Thor himself—could stand in my way from getting back to your side.”

“Oh, Huw,” said Astrid softly, lifting her head to kiss him, losing herself in the intimacy of the moment. *My warrior, and I’m his witch. Nothing could make me happier.*

***

Their journey into the mountains passed without incident. Under Huw’s guidance, they made steady going, and his skill with a snare kept them well fed. With Huw’s permission and careful observation, Astrid was able to find more delicious chanterelle mushrooms to flavor their food. Huw kept a watchful eye out for any other travelers in the mountains, but there were none to be found. Their nights were spent in warm embrace, the sounds of their lovemaking kept carefully low.

Finally, after several days’ steady hiking, Huw carefully ascended a rock promontory, keeping his head low as he scanned his environment. He carefully climbed back down to rejoin Astrid.

"We're close," he said. "Cold camps from now on, unfortunately—we can't risk a fire being seen. We're perhaps a day or so away. Do you see that spur of rock, right against the sky?"

Astrid followed the direction of Huw's pointing finger and nodded. The mountains could be deceptive in distances and landmarks, but the rocky spur was clear.

"Those who know about the hideout call that the Jewel. Like, the jewel in the crown. Bandits and raiders use the Jewel as their guide, and approach from below, the easiest route.

Unfortunately, we can't go that way. Approaching the Jewel from below, you can be spotted a mile off by any watchman, and we can bet they have someone watching."

"Okay," nodded Astrid, "so how do we approach?"

"From above," said Huw, and pointed. Astrid's face fell as she regarded what looked like sheer, unforgiving faces of rock, as upright as walls and seeming as smooth as glass.

Huw chuckled. "Not to fear, my witch. It's nowhere near as bad as it seems. From a distance, it looks impossible and so no one even considers it, but they're wrong. It can be done."

"How can you know that?" asked Astrid.

Huw grinned. "Because I've done it before, of course."

Later that day, when taking a break from their steep climb north of the Jewel, Huw called a break, and as Astrid shrugged off her pack and rested her feet, he approached her with a thin branch in his hand.

"What do you plan to do with that?" Astrid asked uncertainly, and once again Huw laughed.

Astrid had noticed that the closer they came to their dangerous goal, the merrier Huw became.

"A different kind of teaching, my dear. Not for your bottom, but for illustration." He knelt at her feet and used the branch to sketch a quick map.

"It looks like the outline of a bottle," observed Astrid.

Huw nodded. "Very good. It is much like a bottle. The neck," he said, pointing, "is the entrance. Very hard to get through, very easy to defend. As far as they are concerned, the only way in or out. But they're wrong." Huw now pointed to what looked like the base of the bottle. "My way takes us down right to the heart of the encampment. No one guards it because it's thought to be impossible to climb up or down. It's not. We'll have to do the final part in darkness, but it's much easier than anyone imagines."

Astrid looked at him. "How on earth did you ever find this out?"

Huw gave her a cheeky grin yet again. "A misspent youth. More precisely, a dare. I was more careless of my life back then."

Astrid punched him in the arm. "Mind you're not careless of it now!"

"Yes, my witch," he laughed.

The rest of day was spent in a careful ascent, well above the Jewel. Astrid marveled at Huw's ease in navigating the dangerous stretches of slope and scree to get themselves into position.

"You must be half mountain goat," panted Astrid as Huw lifted her over a particularly treacherous-looking boulder.

"The bottom half, if our lovemaking is anything to go by," jested Huw.

Where it not for the risk of alerting those below, Astrid would have thrown a rock at him.

The day's hard travel finally brought them to the lip of a cliff face Huw said would be their descent to the Mountain Crown. They carefully peered over the edge to see the inhabitants of the hidden camp bustling about their business far below.

"They look like ants, moving about in their comings and goings," said Astrid in wonder.

"And the boot is coming, though they do not know it," said Huw with grim humor. "I count between ten and fifteen of them, maybe more hidden away. A challenging task, but not impossible."

"You can't possibly be telling me we'll descend this," said Astrid, gesturing to what seemed like a sheer cliff face.

"Have faith in me, my witch." Huw said with amusement. "I know what it looks like, but its secrets are not unknown to me. Let's wait for nightfall. Under cover of darkness, we'll be at their throats before they are even aware we have arrived."

He moved them back from the edge and sat Astrid down, looking at her sternly. "Now, my witch, I know that we haven't always had the best history on this, but listen to me carefully."

Astrid rolled her eyes.

"Once we start this, I need you to obey me in everything I say. Everything! There will be no time to question or debate. You *must* do exactly as I tell you."

"I understand, Huw," she said quietly

"I will not threaten you with consequences. There is only one consequence. Disobey me once we begin, and it means our deaths. So, I need to make sure that you understand this."

Astrid swallowed. "Yes, Huw."

Huw smiled, and clasped her shoulder. "Good girl. That's the spirit. Once we have finished our descent, I'm going to designate a place for you to wait. If we didn't have to escape through the bottleneck, I'd keep you here and come back for you. But I need you down there with me so we can be out and clear of the Mountain Crown as quick as may be. So, when I tell you to stay in a certain place, *that's exactly what you must do*. Otherwise, I'll leave you here and take the risk of a journey back here to get you. Can you stay where you're told?"

Astrid was beginning to get annoyed. "I heard you the first time!"

Huw's teeth flashed white in the growing darkness. "That's my witch. I would have been worried if you had been too agreeable."

Astrid muttered in exasperation.

Huw settled in to where he was sitting. "Now we wait."

Night fell swiftly in the mountains. The air was clear, and it was not long before the stars appeared in the inky black sky. At this altitude, where the air was thinner, it was filled with their twinkling pinpricks of light. Astrid could smell the smoke of campfires below, and the sound of singing and laughter rose up to their ears.

"The fools," murmured Huw. "They know not what awaits them."

Finally, conversations below began to fall away. As time passed into the deepest portions of the night and began to move toward early morning. Huw got up and began to stretch.

"Give yourself a good stretch, too, Astrid," said Huw softly. As she did so, Huw uncoiled a short length of rope, and wove it into a harness around his waist and shoulders.

"What's that for?" whispered Astrid.

"For carrying you, my witch," replied Huw.

"Oh, no," said Astrid, backing way. "You are *not* carrying me down that cliff like a sack of flour! No, Huw!"

Huw said simply, "You swore obedience. Now follow through."

Astrid closed her eyes, took a breath then opened

them again. "All right."

"Good girl," said Huw. "You can trust me. Now, come here and follow my instructions."

After a few minutes, Astrid was tied securely to Huw's back. Her feet were already off the ground, and she felt incredibly uncomfortable. She could do nothing more than wave her arms and legs.

"All right, my love," said Huw softly. "Trust in my strength. But do me a favor and don't wriggle around."

Astrid felt a rush of warmth at his intimate address then a rush of ice through her veins as Huw swung over the lip of the cliff face and began their descent.

Astrid had to close her eyes and focus on her breathing. Every inch of her wanted to scream, to twist and try to hold onto something, *anything* that could give her some sense of control. She refused to open her eyes again because if she did, she would look down, and if she looked down, she would go mad.

The wind was icy cold against her face as they descended. For his part, Huw was as sure-footed as the mountain goat she had earlier accused him of being. *Gods, his strength is enormous*, thought Astrid, and she took a moment to marvel at what a specimen of a man he was, as he made his way down a cliff in near-total darkness with a person strapped to his back.

It felt like forever to Astrid, helpless on his back, her feet dangling into nothingness, as she listened to the whistling wind, Huw's measured breathing, and the infinitesimally small sounds of Huw changing his grip and footholds as he steadily descended. *This must be the very apex of trust. My life is entirely and completely in his hands.* Whatever Huw's thoughts might have been, he kept them to himself, moving from foothold to foothold, grip to grip, her entire world shrank to the step by step process of navigation he followed.

Finally, Huw settled on firm ground once again. She felt like crying, but could not make a sound. Instead, she and Huw fell to work on the ropes that had secured her to his back. When she was finally released, Huw turned and hugged her fiercely, kissing her forehead and rubbing her back.

Whispering directly into her ear, he said, "That was the bravest thing I've ever seen anyone do. I'm so proud of you."

Even in the cold pre-dawn hours, his words of praise made her feel warm.

Slowly, cautiously, Huw moved forward, Astrid following close behind. The Mountain Crown was a collection of small huts, with a single great hall. In the middle of the enclosure was a pool of water, black as night and reflecting the stars. Against one wall was a stable, and they could see the movement of horses tethered within.

With a few gestures, Huw pointed out where the bottleneck entrance was, and where Astrid should conceal herself while Huw went about his work. He kissed her one last time and moved off into the darkness.

Huw knew that this was going to be a tricky affair--he had to set the tempo of action, and take advantage of the initial confusion his attack would cause. However, if there were things he could accomplish by stealth before that moment came, that was all to the good.

He assumed that they had set a watchman on the Jewel and considered that to be enough, for there were no sentries standing within the enclosure. Leaving the main hall aside for the moment, he moved to one of the huts. Carefully, quietly opening the door, he peered inside to see if it was occupied.

Huw could hear snoring, and as his vision settled, he could see the form of a man sleeping, his body curled around something. A step closer, revealed that it was a wineskin. That would make things easier.

He took a careful look then leapt onto the man's chest, seizing his throat with one hand while pinning the unfortunate fellow's arms with his knees. With his free hand, he set his dagger to the man's neck, just under his jaw. The man's eyes flew wide open, and he struggled briefly in fright then calmed himself at the feel of sharp, cold steel.

"One cry means your death," whispered Huw fiercely. "Do you understand?"

The man nodded and remained motionless.

"Where are the bone wands? Tell me, and I may spare your life," whispered Huw, slowly removing his hand from the fellow's throat.

"One...one is in the main hall, with Sitric," the fellow said, his voice a low rasp.

"And the other?"

"Eirik has the other," the prone man replied. "He is in the hut next to the stable, guarding the witch."

Huw's hand tightened on the man's throat, causing the man's eyes to bug out, then released his grip. "What witch?".

"Some she-bitch he captured from the Ironwood. She is to burn tomorrow. We will consecrate the bone-wands in her fire, then we go to the Ironwood. No one can stop the true *Brennari*!" The man's eyes blazed fiercely as he snarled out the words.

Even speaking of it seemed to have brought the man new courage, and Huw saw him draw breath in preparation for a shout to warn the others. Without hesitation, Huw used his dagger to end the man's life.

Eirik has captured a witch? This bodes ill. Huw he left the hut, stealthy as a cat, and made his way across the enclosure to the second hut, adjacent to the stable.

The hairs on the back of Huw's neck stood up as he approached the door. Something felt very wrong.

Narrowing his eyes, Huw leaned close, his ears straining. Within, he could hear a low muttering. Eirik's voice.

"I hope you're ready for burning, witch. We know how to do it properly. No quick flame, no smoke to choke you unconscious. Oh no, a slow burn, so that you will feel the flesh of your feet melt away, the flames blistering your legs...and as long as I use the *bengand* against you, not a single thing you can do to stop or ease your agony."

"Put that foul thing away, if you're a man. See if you can handle a single helpless woman," came a bitter voice in response.

Soft, sinister laughter from Eirik. "And make myself prey to your foul blood-magic? Not a chance.".

Huw's thoughts were racing. Eirik was awake and aware, and unlikely to be taken by surprise. In turn, he could warn the whole encampment, and there seemed little Huw could do to stop him. But if Huw attacked the hall first, surely Eirik would cut the witch's throat before he did anything else! He was unwilling to doom the woman.

Huw took a deep breath, and, as he did so, he felt a certain kind of calm overtake him. *No one escapes their fate. The gods and goddesses have brought you here, and if you are truly Freyja's agent, it is time to accept that your fate is in her hands.*

Breathing out, Huw, opened the door to the hut and walked in.

"Hello, Eirik," he said. "I have spent a long time, looking for you."

***

Astrid watched carefully from her vantage point amongst the craggy rocks. Although it was dark, the combination of her growing night vision and the gleam of the stars on the pool helped to follow the rough outlines of what was happening. She saw Huw move stealthily to one hut, then there was nothing for a time. Finally, she saw his brawny form move from to another. He crouched at the door for a while, then Astrid watched in astonishment as Huw finally stood up and simply walked inside.

What did this mean? Astrid peered into the night as best she could, but for Huw to simply walk into a hut where she could see light from within, that was beyond her understanding. Had he found someone he knew? She briefly panicked at the thought that all of this had been some kind of elaborate setup, but she quickly dismissed the thought. Astrid had had ample opportunity to take the measure of Huw and knew him for the man he was. No, there must be some other reason for his action, even though she did not yet know what it was.

So, Astrid waited, trusting in her warrior.

***

Huw took in the scene in front of him as he walked in. The hut was a squalid place, with a single straw bed upon which Eirik sat, two or three candles providing illumination, and a young woman, her face dirty and bruised, sitting bound on the dirt floor.

Eirik looked up at Huw's entrance. His face paled briefly then took on a more calculating look. "Huw of

Hestur," he said slowly, "I did not think to find you here."

"I cannot say the same for you," replied Huw. "This is precisely where I thought to find you. It seems you have friends that we at Jomsburg never knew about."

Eirik sneered. "There are a lot of things you never knew about."

Huw nodded gravely. "So, I have been learning." He squatted down between Eirik seat's on the bed, and the bound witch sitting on the floor. "How long have you been part of the *Brennari*?"

"My family has been a part since the very beginning," said Eirik proudly. "We were there when the first witch was burned, and, by Odin, we'll be there for the last one."

"I do not think that Odin would look favorably on what you do," said Huw, trying to keep Eirik's attention focused on his words rather than what his hand was doing where Eirik could not see.

"You only show your ignorance," sneered Eirik. "Have you never listened to the sagas? The gods pierced the witch Gullveig with three spears and held her pinned over a fire until she died. We do the work of the gods!"

"You and that bone wand of yours," prompted Huw.

To Huw's gratification, Eirik pulled the *bengand* out. The man was as much of a showoff and boaster as Huw had remembered.

"That's right, Huw. The bone wand. One of four, crafted with great skill in secret, the seeds of destruction for the bitches and whores of the Ironwood." Eirik's eyes narrowed. "I have been told you have some knowledge of the others. You will tell all, before you die."

Huw shook his head. "I do not think so." He quietly tensed, waiting for his moment. The witch behind him did not move, though surely she had felt him untie the knot that bound her.

Eirik laughed. "You do not know how the tongues of fire can make anyone speak. But you will see."

He opened his mouth to call for others. Huw recognized his moment and took it, rushing forward with tremendous speed.

Eirik's eyes grew wide and he tried to retreat, shouting for aid, but not before Huw managed to seize the bone wand and hurl him to the floor.

Freyja, if I am doing your will, help me now.. He

took the carved and amber-encrusted walrus tusk in both hands and flexed with every ounce of his strength.

For a moment, nothing happened. Then, suddenly, the tusk cracked then split apart, and the whole world went white.

***

Huw opened his eyes and found that he had been flung full length along the ground. Groaning, he looked around him, and saw that instead of the dirt floor of the hut, he was lying in a meadow of long grass and flowers.

A strange feeling of calm washed over him. *I wonder if I have died. I hope Astrid survived. I will wait for her here, until it is her time.* He felt a pang of sadness. *I would have liked to have made children with her, brought them into the world and raised them. I suppose that was too much to hope for.*

"Huw of Hestur," came a voice from behind him, "it seems that you must love my meadow, since you return to it every time you are shaken."

Huw sat up quickly and turned. In front of him was a vision of his true love. Astrid was there, in beautiful and flowing finery, and yet somehow it was *not* Astrid. When he looked into her eyes, he saw something else.

"You are not Astrid," he said flatly.

The vision laughed. "No, I am not. I often appear as someone's true love, however, since I am the embodiment of true love. You are quick to spot the difference, Huw of Hestur."

"I know every part of her," said Huw simply.

"I believe you. Well, Huw, what am I to do with such a brave warrior? You have served me so very well. There are few on Midgard who could have shattered a *bengand*. Your strength is mighty. You would be a mighty addition to my company, as one of my warriors here in Folkvangr."

"That may well be my destiny, when my life's weave has come to a finish," said Huw, "but for now, I ask that you grant me leave to return to Midgard, where my true love waits for me."

Freyja smiled, and a thought struck Huw. "What of the other *bengands*?" he asked suddenly. "I left two with Astrid."

Freyja looked at him, and said, "Four bone wands were made, in secret and in evil. One you shattered, the two you left with Astrid were destroyed in the explosion that followed, and one remains."

"Explosion!" Huw jumped to his feet. "It caused

an explosion? What of Astrid? Is she safe? The other witch? Eirik had a witch bound in the hut. I was trying to save her. I didn't know breaking the *bengand* would lay waste to everything."

"You succeeded saving the life of the witch Eirik threatened. She is safe. Astrid is in a meadow very much like this one, where I am also speaking with her. She has faced the same questions as you: does she wish to remain among the honored host, here in Folkvangr? Does she wish to return to Midgard?"

Huw held his breath. "And what has she answered? What are her wishes?"

Freyja's smile was radiant and filled the meadow. "Her wishes are the same as yours, in every respect," she replied. "Go to her now. Remember, my brave warrior, that your place in the hall of Folkvangr is assured when your days on Midgard are done."

Huw dropped to one knee and humbly inclined his head. "Thank you, great lady. I am in your debt."

Her hand touched his head, like the kiss of a butterfly. "No, Huw of Hestur. The debt is mine. Now, go see your witch."

Even as Huw was about to once again give his thanks, the meadow began to fade away, to be replaced once more with the enclosure of the Mountain Crown.

As he saw it now, however, the Mountain Crown was a scene of utter devastation. It was as if Thor's hammer itself had come down in a mighty, shattering blow, right upon the hut where Huw had confronted Eirik. From that point, a circle of destruction radiated outward, with just a few burn marks to show where there had once been a hall. The majority of the pool had simply evaporated; a much reduced amount of water lying in the bottom of what now appeared to be a rain-filled crater.

A further distance away, kneeling on the ground with her head bowed, was Astrid. Huw shouted for sheer joy.

"Astrid! My love!" He ran toward her, as fast as his legs would carry him. She looked up, dazed, and then her face was transformed by her dazzling smile.

"Huw..." Her face was glowing as Huw closed the distance between them and enveloped her in his embrace.

"Oh, my love, my love..." whispered Huw fiercely into her ear.

"I was with her, Huw! I was with Freyja! She laid her hand on me and offered me a place among the honored spirits at Folkvangr. But I didn't want to be without you, my warrior! I asked to come back here, to be with and build a life with you."

"I know, my witch, I know. Freyja told me all. Her favor saved us and has given us the opportunity to build a life together. It's all I want, Astrid. I want us to see our children grow up and laugh and play in the home we build for ourselves."

"The mighty Jomsviking wants little children of his own?" teased Astrid, her hand on his chest.

Huw grinned. "Well, we'll need to work hard on getting you with child, but I guess that's just a price we'll have to pay."

Astrid's laughter rang through the mountains, and somewhere far away, Freyja looked down and smiled upon her chosen.

Curious to know if Brynn survives and returns to the Ironwood to claim Kasia? Then look for BONE AND BLADE releasing the Summer of 2021:

Pain—deep and sharp. Brynn found it hard to breathe. Was he dying? It felt like he should be dying. But where were the Valkyries? Where were the gates to Valhalla? Surely, he had earned his place at the great table.

Treachery. It surrounded him. One of his brothers had tried to end his life. Eirik. Oathbreaker.

And the witch...the witch who had stolen his seed. Had it taken root? Didn't she know they were meant to be together? She was his; he would claim her...but first he would take a strap to her backside and leave welts behind. Arousal surged through him. Could a man be facing death and feel his cock rising? She was beautiful—his witch, his woman. Yes, he would welt her, and then he would fuck her on her knees, breaching her with his cock and thrusting into her over and over, his pelvis butting her red and heated backside...a most satisfying fuck. And he would have her again and again, and she would bear him many sons.

The vision faded just as he heard her cry out his name in surrender and ecstasy. He would make it come to pass. This he vowed. Brynn felt the warmth of the fire in the cool night as his eyes fluttered open.

Other books by Delta James:

https://www.deltajames.com/

Want FREE books from Delta James?

Go to https://www.subscribepage.com/VIPlist22019 to sign up for Delta James' newsletter and receive free stories. In addition to the free stories you will also get access to bonus stories, sales, giveaways and news of new releases.

About Delta James

If you're looking for paranormal, dark and contemporary western erotic romance, you've found your new favorite author!

Alpha heroes find real love with feisty heroines in Delta James' sinfully sultry romances. Welcome to a world where true love conquers all and good triumphs over evil! Delta's stories are filled with erotic encounters of romance and discipline.

About Tom Rhymer

I've been in love with stories my entire life, and now I'm finally creating them!

I started writing in order to be able to read the sort of stories I wanted. With my love of romantic stories (of course with a dark edge to them), I wanted to explore the possibilities of mixing classic themes with the darker side of erotica.

I invite you to come and escape with me into the worlds I make—some are entirely my own, and some might look similar to things you know!

Website: tomrhymer.com

FB: https://www.facebook.com/TheRhymersCourt

IG: tom.rhymer

Made in the USA
Monee, IL
11 March 2022

92744235R00156